MIAOW THERE!
IT'S STILL MISTY OUT AT SEA

THE CELEBRITY CAT'S LATEST (B)LOG

BY SHEILA COLLINS
FOREWORD BY ANN WIDDECOMBE

APEX PUBLISHING LTD

First published as an eBook in 2016.
First published in paperback in 2016 by

Apex Publishing Ltd

12A St. John's Road, Clacton on Sea, Essex, CO15 4BP, United Kingdom

www.apexpublishing.co.uk

British Library Cataloguing-in-Publication Data
A catalogue record for this book
is available from the British Library

ISBN: 978-1-911476-35-1

Typeset in 12.5pt Palatino Linotype

Production Manager: Chris Cowlin
Cover Designer: Hannah Blamires

AUTHOR'S NOTE

Misty's second book describing her adventures on a trip to The Azores and The Canary Islands is set once more on my own favourite cruise ship. In her first book I added a few extra 'frills' from another great ship I've travelled on … to show, as an example to those of you who haven't yet joined the millions of us who love cruising, even more of the fantastic facilities you will come across on the many wonderful palaces on the sea that we have today. So, to all you non-cruisers, you simply must try a cruise for yourselves. I'm sure Misty would be delighted if you did!

This time, however, no extras have been added but I hope from Misty's descriptions, fellow passengers will recognise the ship in question and hopefully have a few smiles at her take on things and feel a sense of déjà vu.

Of course, as readers of my books will know, I write looking at the world through a cat's eyes (ha ha!) but obviously I didn't actually bring a cat on board…

Anyway, I hope you enjoy!

FOREWORD BY ANN WIDDECOMBE

Followers of Misty will love this adventure – from her chivalrous attempt to save a bullied ball and the dubious thrill of a ride down a steep hill on a wicker toboggan, to the beguiling ways with the room steward to secure those tempting shrimps…

www.apexpublishing.co.uk

LET ME INTRODUCE MYSELF!

Hello people!

It's Misty here again and I do hope you enjoyed reading about my adventures on a fabulous cruise ship last summer. From a cat's point of view, I couldn't have thought of anything worse than being surrounded by water, water everywhere but my 'purrsonal' assistant and housekeeper, Sheila, loves going on her cruises so much (56 to date!) that my cat's curiosity got the better of me and when she got an invite for me to accompany her I – almost – jumped at the chance. My predecessor, Truffles, a well-known cat author, had also been on the same ship and written a book about it which I believe you cat and cruise loving humans enjoyed. Truffles told me how exciting a journey it had been but sadly she later took the final journey we all dread … to that giant cat basket in the sky … so I decided to follow in her pawprints.

On the ship I might say – I'm not ready to go aloft yet!

Much to my surprise I really, really enjoyed the whole experience. So, this year I've done it all again but this time I knew what to expect and how best to use my cat skills in getting the crew on board to pamper to my every whim. Well, after all, the old adage is totally correct – humans have bosses, dogs have masters and cats have servants!

So, put your paws up and read on.

PREPARATIONS

As per usual, it took Sheila about three weeks to decide what clothes to wear and what paw covers (sorry, you call them shoes!) to take, let alone all the sparkly stuff she wears round her neck and wrists and the ridiculous number of bags she carries. All this gear took up three large cases and I have to say when I heard her panting and struggling to drag them to the hallway, muttering those words a well brought up little cat does NOT want to hear, I had to give an inward grin and think, well dear you brought it on yourself! If you wore a nice, fully fitted, fur catsuit like I do, there's nothing else to take when you travel except a selection of collars ... much more sensible and the added bonus of being light to carry. Think on!

I have to say that you humans do have some strange habits when it comes to trying to make yourselves more attractive. For example, why do you male humans shave off your face fur and whiskers? No self-respecting cat (or dog for that matter) would ever do that. YOU select your kitten or puppy for its pretty fur and cute whiskers which is generally the main thing that attracts you to it at first sight. And why do you lady humans forever want to change your fur (hair, sorry!) colour, surround your eyes with black fringes and paint lurid colours on your claws? Ah well, we cats will never understand your habits, but then I guess you will never understand ours either.

Eventually, Sheila had packed all her stuff and also mine ...

evening collars, day collars, brush and comb, food, bed, litter box and sack of cat litter – oh dear, I'd better shut up about being overloaded as when it came down to it, I had almost as much stuff to carry as she did! Not that it mattered really because a charming, long-suffering guy called Tony, who drives us to the port, would do all the carrying anyway. The ship lives in the port of Southampton for the summer each year so that's where we were headed. I remember that last time we met some people on board who lived in a place called Northampton. I wonder if there is an Easthampton and a Westhampton anywhere? We live in Cornwall ourselves … being a curious cat, I've often wondered if there's a Haywall, Oatwall or even a Ryewall anywhere too. But enough of my mewsings – I'm sure you're all wanting to hear about the cruise, so I'll get on with it.

DAY 1

Sheila got up at the unearthly hour of 6.00 a.m. so I was rudely awakened about 10 minutes later. Nuisance because I had got to the spot in a nice dream I was having where I was about to catch a bird. I have to say that I'm a bit ashamed (as a cat!) to admit that I have never caught a bird in my entire life. Generally being of a shy disposition, I've always been rather scared that I would get my eyes pecked out. Yes, I know I am a wimp in the killing fields but at least I can blow my own trumpet and say that not every cat becomes an author. I can keep my feline end up, though, by saying that I have caused the decease of quite a few spiders and even the odd daddy-long-legs.

By 6.45 a.m. we were in a state of anticipation waiting for Tony to arrive. A pile of Sheila's suitcases plus my various bags lay waiting for him in the hall. I hoped he would be feeling strong so early in the day. Dead on time he arrived and he looked very different from the last time we saw him. He must have read my mind about you men humans and your face fur or lack of it. He was sporting a full brown beard, albeit with a few grey bits sprinkled in it. He looked much better I thought, and gave him an appreciative rub round the ankles, unfortunately leaving some more grey bits (fur from me) on his smart trousers. But I don't think he noticed ... Sheila also made a comment that he looked very trendy. He, and all the drivers from his taxi company, always look smart and tidy. (It's called A and J but I don't know what that means – maybe Automan + Jalopy? I think you have a hero called Superman like we cats have our hero Top Cat. Superman wears trendy shorts with a vest with the letter 'S' on it. Maybe Tony and his drivers should wear similar apparel with the letters 'A' and 'J' on their vests!). Anyway, whatever they wear they get you to your destination right on time so that's why Sheila has been a regular customer for so long. And I am now becoming a regular too! After a bit of heaving and hauling, the luggage and me were stowed in the taxi, Sheila locked the front door, got in herself and settled me down on her thighs (sorry dear, I know you don't like people to notice your well upholstered thighs, but to me they're like sitting on a pair of comfy cushions!) and off we went. Southampton docks here we come!

On my road trip last year I was all agog at what we passed. The animals in the fields, the oh, so many birds flying about or perched on those odd poles stuck up along the roadside, let alone all the – sometimes to a small cat like me – scary, huge, noisy motor machines thundering past. But as I said at the start, this trip I knew what to expect and those motors hadn't harmed us so I felt much more confident than before. In fact, I was totally looking forward to experiencing even more things on this trip. I knew that this time Sheila was going to be taking me ashore at some of the ports we would call at. My cat passport was all in order and I had been given a few extra jabs at the vet's so I was all ready for the off.

After we had driven down the road and I'd been looking out of the window for a while, I heard Tony say, "So, where are you off to this time, eh?"

To which Sheila replied, "First stop will be at The Azores."

'The Azores?' I'd never heard that word before … what on earth is an 'azore'? Although, of course, I can't speak in your language, as a writer and listener I know lots of your words and I must say your human vocabulary certainly puts my powers of understanding fully to the test. Oh well, you learn something new every day, so soon I would know what an 'azore' is.

"Then we are at Madeira," continued Sheila. Oh well, I know what that is, I thought, a cake! So I suppose at our first stop we will be looking at an 'azore' (whatever that turns out to be) and then eating cake. That would be nothing out of the ordinary for Sheila – she is always eating cakes. Myself, I stay away from them – I prefer nice fishy crunchy treats. And then she went on, "Next we are at the Canary Islands, going to four of them before going home via Lisbon."

"Oh, that'll be exciting for Misty with all those birds around," said Tony.

"Stop winding her up," said Sheila with a giggle. 'Wind me up'? What were they on about now, I'm not a clock! BUT – I sat bolt upright, canaries? Oh my, now that really does sound exciting! I remember one of the cats next door telling me it had seen a canary in a cage once, a little yellow bird that chirped and fluttered in a most appealing way. And we were going to four places FULL of these little birds? Oh my! That would be something, I could boast about to the other cats when we got home. I lay back down again with pleasant images of hundreds of little yellow birds flying all round me, tempting me from every direction, though sadly with my past record of being a non-bird catcher, I guess I wouldn't be able to catch one.

It seemed quite a long time before we stopped. I had alternately dozed or looked out at the scenery whizzing past. The lovely milk-giving cows and the woolly animals I don't know the names of looked happy enough in their lush green fields and there were plenty of pretty birds twittering and flying around the hedges and trees. I remembered on my last drive to Southampton seeing a very, very large bird (I think Sheila and Tony called it a buzzbird or something that sounded like that) sitting on one of those big roadside poles and it looked pretty scary. It was ENORMOUS, like something out of a horror film for cats. But fortunately, on this trip, I didn't see another one. Tony and Sheila got out of the motor machine and we walked over to some tables and chairs that were set outside a building from which came the smell of that frothy coffee which you humans love but which I find somewhat sweet and repulsive. I prefer the smell of a nice, day old, piece of fish.

I would have liked to have wandered off whilst they sat and drank their coffee but I was in the humiliating position (for a cat) of having a lead attached to my collar to which Sheila held on firmly. I hate having to wear such a thing … after all I am NOT a dog … but I had it drummed into me last time that in no way would I be allowed onto the ship or, indeed, into the port without one. So I had to get over it and just count my blessings that the cruise line seemed to like me and was happy for me to return. I've had it explained to me often enough by Sheila how lucky I am to go on a ship … something that just doesn't generally happen to cats! And from the comments she gets from people who read my books, I guess that's true and so I might as well bask in my five minutes of fame … and in the sunshine here outside the coffee place.

The sound of Sheila and Tony nattering, plus the warm sunshine, made me doze off quite quickly and I was only awakened when I felt a slight tug on the lead and realised that Sheila had passed it over to Tony and was walking alone into the building. I wondered why … I remember this had happened last time – she had gone off for about five minutes and then come out and taken hold of me whilst he had gone in and disappeared for about five minutes. I wondered what they had been doing. Tony bent down and patted me and I gave him a nice purr and another ankle rub. Whoops, more grey fur on his immaculate black trouser legs, but he still hadn't noticed because it was at the back. Anyway, at least both legs matched now, plain on the front and fur trimmed on the back. Sheila returned, he then disappeared and then a few minutes later out he came and we were off again.

"We've made excellent time," remarked Tony, "but it could all go pear-shaped when we get near the docks because the Boat Show is on this weekend."

"And," said Sheila, "it also depends on how many other cruise ships are in today, but it doesn't matter, we're nice and early." Oh well, time to finish my nap then, I thought … over and out.

A while later, I awoke and could see that we were near the

port. On each side of the road were huge metal monsters that were slowly carrying, what looked to me, like massive tin boxes, others were rising into the air with these same things dangling from their necks – like giant metal giraffes, I thought. Slowly, following a line of other motor machines, we eventually arrived at a gateway guarded by an official looking human in uniform. Oh dear, I remembered that last time we reached here the official was most rude referring to me as 'What's that? You can't bring that here!' I'm a cat, not a 'that' and I was ready to give him a hiss and a scratch to prove it but Sheila calmed the situation down by producing documents proving that I was a guest of the ship and that shut him up. So, I prepared for action. But this time it was a different man and he was all smiles and when he saw me he just laughed.

"Fancy seeing a cat coming on a cruise," he said, "for pleasure, or is she a guide cat like we get guide dogs sometimes?"

"No," replied Sheila, "she's a travel writer. She's never been a guide." That made him laugh even more.

"If she wasn't a guide, maybe she was in the cubs then?" he said. By this time the guard, Sheila and Tony were all making that awful screeching sound you humans call laughing, sounding like a group of our cat cousins, the hyenas, but at least he waved us through with none of the unpleasantness we'd had last year.

Reaching the side of the ship, which always looks like a mountain with windows to a small (no, in my case petite!) cat person like me, Tony unloaded our bags and they were immediately taken away by one of the many carrying men (porters I think you call them) and I hoped they would find the way to our cabin and not get lost. In no way did I wish to lose my comfy bed or my collection of fancy collars. Sheila thanked Tony who gave me a last pat, told us to enjoy ourselves and drove off smiling. His smile might have dropped when he inspected his trouser legs later!

We entered the building by the ship, Sheila dragging along a case on wheels, plus carrying a big paw bag – sorry, handbag – and somehow managing to keep a firm grip on my lead too. Pity that. Last time I was nervous and wanted to stay right by her side, but now that I was much more confident I would have liked to have had more of a look around at so many things that I just don't see where we live. So many people of all shapes, colours and sizes speaking in so many different accents, some looking very excited, some looking quite stressed or tired but all headed in the same direction … TO THE SHIP! Walking behind the crowd we approached the line of check in desks with more people in smart uniforms sitting behind them. At the front a lady human was asking people which CATegory of guest they were (that's a nice feline touch I thought) and Sheila told her that she was Elite Plus. So she was given a red sticker and we followed a relatively small number of people to the first available desk. The lady behind it smiled and said she had been alerted that a cat guest was expected and so when she said she was taking Sheila's photo for ID purposes, (I don't know what ID means, maybe 'idiot'? Sorry, Sheila dear, only joking!) she took mine too. Oh well, if she took MY photo it certainly didn't mean 'idiot' because that word definitely does not describe cats!

Next stop was at that weird place where they put all your bags into a moving tunnel, look at them through some magic camera that shows up everything inside and if you have nothing naughty in them, you can pick them up again and carry on. When we came here before I was scared they'd put ME into the tunnel but thankfully they didn't. Well, I guess they could see that I wasn't carrying anything I shouldn't. Sheila obviously wasn't carrying anything she shouldn't either (except maybe some excess weight ... sorry dear!) so we soon passed through a narrow archway which was, I noticed, squeaking when some people went under it, and out of that area.

Anyway, all the checking in processes now being complete, there was another long trek through the building and up in a lift to the floor above. I would have liked to have gone up the moving staircase but that proved a no-no as with me, her case and her handbag Sheila couldn't cope. I also reminded myself I must call lifts elevators when on the ship, and our cabin a stateroom. Can't remember why exactly, but last time I was on it somebody said the ship is 'a merry can', or some word that sounded like that, and people on it use a few different words from us. Come to think of it most people are thrilled to be on the ship and ARE merry so perhaps it's an apt description! As I've said before the world outside Cornwall is a massive, difficult to understand, and sometimes frightening place for a little cat like me to take in. But at least I know I can impress the next door cats. I've had the chance to travel the world; they've never even been out of our street. Paws up to me!

After zigzagging up a long and quite steep covered-in

pathway, we finally reached the entrance to the ship. Sheila had some sticky stuff sprayed onto her hands but luckily nobody put such stuff on my paws. If they had of done, I would have definitely given them a scratch. Yuk, I can't stand anything sticky on my fur. Yet another machine loomed up and the man in charge swiped our stateroom card through it making a satisfactory pinging sort of sound, rather like a fat, furry mouse would make when grabbed tightly by a cat. Again, much like those tantalizing little birds, I've never caught a mouse either so I haven't personally experienced the sound. A few steps more and yippee, we were on board. My adventure was about to begin. A nice smiley lady handed Sheila a glass of that bubbly drink she likes, and holding that in one hand, manipulating me and the luggage somehow in the other, she sat down in a luxurious chair, raised the glass and said, "Cheers Misty! We're both going to have fun and you will soon be meeting my friends again on this lovely ship. And talk of the devil, here's one of them coming along now!"

I looked up and saw a tall male human walking towards us with a big grin on his face. He was dressed in a navy blue jacket with gold stripes round the cuffs. "Now behave Misty," said Sheila "here comes Darren, he is high up the tree here as he is the hotel director, so sit nice and quietly." I had a good look at Darren as he approached us and thought he looked nice and as if he probably liked cats and dogs. As I recall, he didn't have as many rings on his sleeves as Dimitrios whom I met last time, but I think Sheila said that HE was the real Top Cat on this ship! Whatever, Darren looked just as smart so I thought I'd better not rub round his ankles if he gave me a pat.

"Well, good to see you back again, Sheila," he said.

"Likewise," she replied.

They chatted for a few minutes and then he looked down at me and said, "Well, how are you Misty? I've heard all about you and I have got your first book (not that I've had time to read it yet because I'm always so busy) but I definitely will when I go home on leave." Oh yes, promises, promises I thought! "And now I hear you are writing another one. Great! I love cats." Oh good I thought, he may make promises he won't keep but I read him correctly – he IS a cat lover. So, I looked up at him and gave him my best pussy smile and a purr and in turn he leaned down and gave me a pat and a tickle behind the ears. Lovely, but I kept well away from his ankles.

"Yes," he continued, "I have a purple Persian cat who we all love and he is definitely the boss of the house." Of course he is, I thought. All cats rule the humans (and dogs) in their home.

"Well," said Sheila, "I've never heard of a purple Persian, ever! I do know there are blue Persians but purple, are you sure?" I must say I have never heard of coloured Persians either. But maybe somewhere there are blue, purple, pink and yellow ones – all sorts of colours. They're not in Cornwall at any rate. In fact, I have never met any cats that weren't black, grey, brown, ginger or white. Certainly, the four Persians who once lived next door to us were normal cat colours. I have to say that, to be honest, I was always a bit wary of them as they were about three times my size (hey, remember I am petite!) and they did tend to gang up and chase me round the garden sometimes. Darren and Sheila spent the next five minutes bantering about purple Persians and then he gave me a final pat and went off to find his crewmate, Guy, who apparently Sheila also seemed to know. It seemed he worked in guest relations – another strange human description. The only relations I have ever heard of are aunts and uncles, mothers and fathers, brothers and sisters. Still, as I know so well, you learn something new every day when you mix with the human race. I looked forward to meeting this guy called Guy during the cruise, as I heard Darren tell Sheila that he too was a cat lover and had several cats of his own.

Sheila polished off the rest of her glass of bubbly and then gathered up the case on wheels and her bag, yanked on my lead and we walked off to where there were a group of lifts (sorry, elevators!) waiting to take us to our stateroom which apparently was way up on Deck 11. There were already quite a few of our fellow passengers in it but somehow we managed to squeeze in. I waited for the usual comments (having heard them all before when I was on the ship). Things like … 'Goodness is that a cat?', 'I didn't know cats went on cruises!', 'I've only had one drink but is that a cat I can see?', 'Can't believe there's a cat on here, aaah!', 'How cute, a cruising cat!', 'Hello puss – have you just come off a catamaran?' But everyone seemed very friendly and nobody said anything nasty or catty (excuse the pun!). The unseen lady who seems to control all the elevators announced that we were at Deck 11 and the doors were opening. I reminded myself that I must try and find the mysterious lady on this trip. I had no success last time and it was really frustrating. She seemed to be in every elevator we went in – and believe you me there are a lot of them on this enormous ship! Her legs must have been so tired at the end of the day running from elevator to elevator(!) and I reckon she must have had a sore throat too, speaking non-stop all day. Anyway, yet another human puzzle for me to solve. Ah well, we got out and made our way towards our stateroom which Sheila told me was very near the back (stern she called it, though I thought the ship seemed very happy actually – not in the least stern!) so there would be no need for her to go to the gym as she would get all her exercise walking to and from our 'home' on board. Well, any excuse, dear, to avoid the dreaded gym!

Well, it did seem quite a long trek but eventually we arrived outside our stateroom and Sheila slipped the magic card into the slot, the door opened and in we went, her to park the case on wheels and sink down on the sofa, me to flop down at her feet. We sat there for a few minutes and then she opened the glass door on to the balcony and I went out to look around whilst she unpacked stuff and fussed around generally. Wait until the main baggage arrives, dear … you'll regret bringing so much when you have to unfold it all and hang it up! I've said it before and I'll say it again, one fully fitted, fur catsuit for all occasions is all we cats need.

The first time I came on the ship I was petrified when I went out on the balcony and saw that we were surrounded by all that water – definitely not an element that cats like in the slightest, except for Turkish Van cats who for some obscure reason love it.

It took all my courage to get myself to the edge and look down and, even now, I remember how my legs went wobbly. But now all that fear was in the past and today I looked eagerly around me at the sunlight glinting on the water (yes, dear reader, SUN, that yellow thing hanging in the sky which we haven't seen much of so far this year in Cornwall!). Sheila had said that there should be a big yellow sun shining over the Canaries so I looked forward to an overdose of yellow; the sun itself and all those bewitching little canary birds flying about under it. Over at the other side of the water I could see those giant metal giraffes in action still, and another ship, but not as big or as nice looking as ours, parked alongside them. Those raucous, noisy, white sea birds were flying about overhead too. Definitely too large for little me to handle, though not quite as scary as those buzz birds. Three of them appeared to be having a tussle over a large fish one of them was holding in its beak. Well, I guess we have something in common ... we all like fish. I was looking forward to room service and being able to get the finest salmon, prawns and crab, like I did last time. I hoped our steward was as nice as the last one who, luckily for me, was a cat lover. It didn't take too much purring and ankle rubbing to get him exactly where I wanted him, under my paw.

Talking of stewards, suddenly there was a knock at the stateroom door which Sheila opened and a smiley steward appeared. "Hello, Madam," he said, "my name is Del and I am going to be looking after you. I hear we have a very special guest called Mistee." He smiled down at me and continued to Sheila, "Is there anything I can get you? Your baggage will be here very soon." Well, he looks nice I thought, it won't take much to charm a few shrimps and chicken bits out of HIM! So I walked up to him, sat down, put on my cutest expression and went into purr mode.

"Ello, Mistee," he said patting my head, "I was told you would be here so I brought you this leetle treat." And, as if he'd read my mind, he gave me a lovely pink shrimp. Oh wow, we're on to a good thing here, I thought. Whilst I demolished the shrimp Sheila said goodbye to Del and continued putting her stuff away. I wandered over to the bathroom – which didn't have a bath in it, so I shall now refer to it as the 'non' bathroom. Yes, so I went into the non-bathroom and looked at the devil incarnate … a cruise ship's water box. We cats do our business in nice quiet litter boxes if there is no access to a handy flower bed in the garden, but you humans determinedly use noisy water boxes at home. Why, I just don't know! Another strange human custom I suppose. But the water boxes on ships beat all with their sudden violent 'swoosh' that sounds like an explosion in a firework factory (another place that would be petrifying to a cat!). Now, of course, I am OK with it – though still a bit wary – but the first time I encountered that ghastly contraption, Sheila, realising I might be scared, took me to look at it, warning me that it was noisy, but harmless. When she had pressed the button to demonstrate I nearly had a heart attack and scarpered as fast as I could under the bed! It took a lot of persuasion from Sheila to get me out and assure me that the nightmare water box wasn't going to swallow me right up. Needless to say, I kept my distance from then on and still will.

Another knock at the door heralded the arrival of our main baggage, so with three large cases to unpack, that would keep Sheila occupied for quite a while. Firstly, though, there was my stuff to put in place. My (quiet) litter box was put neatly into the corner of the balcony with the sack of cat litter and disposal bags close beside it. This cruise company is most particular about elf and safety matters, hyge … hygi … hyegen … sorry … 'er, cleanliness, and actually so is Sheila at home. Well, as she is employed as my purrsonal full-time cleaner and housekeeper I wouldn't have it any other way. She fully understands the job description I gave her, performing her duties up to my required high standards and I knew she would carry them out just the same on the ship and clean up immediately I required her to. I made a note to test her right away and as soon as the box was in place I accordingly performed on it – which was quite a relief anyway since my last performance was at about 6.00 a.m.!

My comfy bed was placed just inside the glass doors and my furry cushion at the foot of the sofa. Right, just as I wanted! So, leaving madam to carry on sorting out her clothes and bits and pieces, I settled down, switched to sleep mode and decided to take a cosy catnap!

Some while later, I was awakened by a voice coming from out of nowhere that I thought I remembered … was it Sue – the cruise director with the fab shoes that Sheila envied so – who had been on when I was here last year? It sounded like her. She didn't have a Cornish accent, or Sheila's London accent, but from somewhere further north I think. She was saying that it would soon be time for lifeboat drill. I got ready to prepare myself for some piercing shrieks from the ship's whistle – another scary noise, like the sound of the water box, that shook me rigid when I heard it for the first time. With the dreaded lead fixed to my collar again, Sheila opened the door and out we went along the passageway to the elevators, but this time nobody was using them and we had to walk down six flights of stairs (wonder why they call them 'flights' ... that's a word that makes me think of birds!). We joined lots of other passengers who were sitting in a beautiful dining room which, on normal occasions, I would never be allowed in (elf and safety again!) so I looked around with interest and marvelled at the glittering lights hanging down in clusters from the ceiling, the elaborate tables and chairs and the glamour of it all. Bit different from being at home!

Whilst we were waiting for the scary emergency whistle to sound and for the lifeboat drill to start – I've heard that dentists have drills, and road workers have drills but I never knew until I came on here last year that ships had drills too – Sheila got chatting to the people sitting next to us and I basked in the attention of the other people nearby who were making the usual cat comments and a couple of them even came and patted me. Oh, I DO like all this attention, I could get used to this! I'm not going to go on and on about the actual drill, and neither am I going to describe every detail of the ship again because, of course, I wrote it all before in my first book and you should have already read it. And slapped wrists all round if you didn't. I don't want to repeat myself and write the same stuff all over again and bore you. No, on this trip I plan to look out for different things to tell you about. Even though I was expecting it, I nearly jumped out of my fur coat when the whistle sounded and some people nearby were putting their paws (sorry, hands) up to their ears. Then Sue's voice came on again and a film started on those big screens on the walls, though I couldn't see it myself as I was sheltering behind

Sheila's ankles ... yes, I'm still a wimp when a very loud noise happens like fireworks, thunder and now the ship's whistle. It goes back to when I was just a youngster and my original owners moved house and there was still a lot of building of other nearby houses going on. There were some very loud, frightening noises, so I totally freaked out. My owners didn't try to comfort me as Sheila would have done, but simply took me out one night and put me on a rubbish tip where I was later found by someone and taken to a cats' home. Anyway, I don't want to think back to those days and dwell on the matter. Sheila came along and we gelled right away and now I've been with her for seven years and she is happy to be my companion, housekeeper and secretary, so how your life can turn around, eh? And now, here I am something of a celebrity in the cat writing world, swanning around on a luxury ship and living like a queen. Unbelievable! But enough of all this, let's get on...

Eventually the film ended and everybody got up and started to go back to their staterooms. There was quite a crowd so there was something of a traffic jam and no chance whatsoever of getting a place in an elevator, so we walked up the six flights of stairs to Deck 11 again. Well, I could have skipped up in half a minute but Sheila was gasping after just three flights.

"Blimey, it's better going down," she said. You should take more exercise dear! Try the gym this time, don't make excuses that all you need to do to keep fit is to walk to and from the stateroom! Eventually, we made it back to the stateroom and she sat down on the sofa and poured out a glass of bubbly. "Come on Misty," she said, "we're about to leave so let's go out on the balcony and say goodbye to Southampton." Out we went and I could hear jolly music coming from above, the people next door to us were also out on their balcony and so everybody raised their glasses, the ship made that sort of barking noise ships make to announce they are departing, then it slowly left the dockside and I was off on my next big adventure!

Sheila went in and finished her unpacking and I sat and watched the sun shining on the water around us. Quite a lot of those big white birds accompanied us on our way but then they got distracted by a smaller boat coming in which smelled of fish (quite made my mouth water!) and left us. The nice perfume of fish made me feel hungry and Sheila must have read my mind because she said it was time for my dinner. "Now," she pondered, "I wonder what you would like, how about some nice bits of chicken breast in gravy and maybe salmon in sauce for a starter?" Mmmm, that sounds OK, I thought, and it will be top notch on here – better than that stuff she gets in pouches from the supermarket. This ship is well known for its top class nosh for you humans and, although they had never catered for a cat guest before I first came on board, they certainly stepped up to the mark. So, I was looking forward to gourmet meals and service to match on this trip. Purring with anticipation I watched as Sheila picked up that little machine you talk into and ordered my dinner. Not very long after it arrived with another smiling steward and, whilst I tucked in, Sheila got herself all dolled up saying we were going to the theatre to watch the early opening show before she had her own dinner as her friend Peng Fei was performing in it.

Ah yes, I remembered him. A lovely guy, though apparently

from China so I was always a bit nervous in case he cracked or shattered or something, but although he performed quite dangerous acrobatics so far he hadn't smashed himself up and still remained in one piece. He was also a brilliant magician and last time he had done a great trick especially for me with three cups and a ball. He'd moved them all around and challenged me to find the ball. Though I was pawsitive I would find the ball, do what I might I just couldn't – it sure WAS magic. Because my eyes are pretty damn sharp I can tell you.

Now that Sheila was dressed up to the nines, it was my turn to get dressed up to the maybe one and a halfs(!) so she picked out one of my evening collars; pale pink with sparkly studs, clipped on its matching lead and off we went along the, by now familiar, passageway to the elevators. There were no crowds of people waiting now so it was easy to get in one. The mysterious unseen lady announced we were at Deck 5 (I'll track her down one day, I vowed) and off we walked towards the front (sorry, bow) end of the ship where the big theatre was situated. On the way we passed by the coffee lounge that Sheila so liked. She does love that brown frothy stuff. Simple, cool, white milk suits cats and is much more healthy. I don't know what you all see in the hot brown stuff you seem to drink in the days, let alone the sickly smelling and white, yellow or red stuff you seem to like in the evenings which makes some of you drunk, stupid and giggly and others sometimes quite punchy and stroppy. Each to his own, I guess. As we passed by the coffee place Sheila stopped and said hi to a couple of the guys there she seemed to know, and that we'd see them later on. I have always been allowed into this coffee lounge if I am well behaved (What!

Would I, Misty, ever misbehave? Whatever gave them that idea?). Because of elf and safety I can never go to any of the eating places you go to which is why I always have room service and eat in the stateroom. But on this second trip, so Sheila told me, because I have shown that I AM well behaved, and I AM a celebrity, I will be allowed to go with her to the bars where she will have those sickly drinks she likes. She calls them cocktails … I've always thought that actually they must taste of chicken so I probably would like them, but I don't want to take the risk of ending up drunk and stupid! I must tell you, though, dear reader that, to my knowledge, Madam has never herself ended up drunk or stupid … yet!

Further along the passageway we passed several shops that had lots of sparkly stuff in their windows and those time telling machines that you wear on your arms. There were shops full of handbags – oh dear, I expect one or two will end up in our baggage when we go home – and another one with men's clothes in it. Then a large one full of that sweet smelling stuff you spray yourselves with (never appealed to me as I prefer the odour of fish and mice) and then we arrived at the theatre.

I remembered being here before when there had been a man standing on the stage talking and everybody had been laughing at him. How embarrassing for him, I really felt sorry for him. Fancy having everyone laugh at you … they hardly let him get a sentence out before they started off. I hope nobody ever laughs at me like that. I couldn't see him anywhere tonight though – perhaps he wouldn't be there this time after the awful experience he must have had before. We were sitting on the top floor of the theatre, there were lots of people round us (those nearby making the usual cat comments) and I could see that all the seats below us were filled too. Sheila settled into her seat with me on her knee (she'd given me a quick brush earlier as she didn't want a fur trim on her outfit!) and soon the lights dimmed and Sue came onto the stage looking very glamorous in a sparkly flowing outfit and wearing her trademark, sparkly, high heels. Bet Sheila fancies them, I thought, but in no way could she balance on them. Sue chattered on about things I wasn't really interested in and then the music began and some singers and dancers appeared also looking very glamorous in sparkly outfits. So slim, full of energy (I bet Sheila wishes she could say that!) and they danced at top speed for several minutes non-stop. So everyone was clapping and cheering and there were a few whistles at the pretty girls (not birdlike!) from some of the men in the audience. Then Sue came on again and announced that Peng Fei was now coming on to perform his renowned ancient Chinese face changing act. I sat up. Yes, of course, I had seen him do it before last time, but how on earth does he do that? Even with my sharp eyes I couldn't see. This time I intended to watch him every second to see just how he did it. I wouldn't have recognised him as he was dressed in some kind of flowing robe with dragon designs on it and he wafted around the stage and, somehow, every few moments he would sweep his arm across and yes his face changed. I know that sounds ridiculous but that's exactly what happened. He must have done it at least ten times and even walked right up to the people sitting in the seats on the lower floor of the theatre and did it literally in front of their eyes and even they couldn't see how he did it. Sheila told me later that it was a traditional kind of Chinese act that was passed down through the generations and a great secret. Peng Fei had been practising it since he was a child she said and was acknowledged to be one of the best. He was always rehearsing and strived for purrfection she said. Well, I knew that because his magic tricks were unbelievable too. And he then did some of those tricks after the face changing. When he finally finished the applause and whistles were deafening and everyone trooped out of the theatre with baffled looks on their faces. We headed back to the stateroom.

Sheila unclipped the lead and said I should curl up have a nap because she was going for her dinner and would be back later to collect me so we could go to the coffee place. That suited me, so off she went. Good, I thought, I'll just pop into the non-bathroom and have a good old claw scratch on the nice fluffy towels in there. I would have to be careful because when I did that last time I got told off in no uncertain terms. This time I would make sure I used the side of the towel hanging against the wall so she and Del wouldn't notice. When he came to tidy up and change the towels he would just screw them up anyway to take away. And I'm happy to report to you, dear reader, that this strategy worked for the whole trip…

Yes Sheila – you never knew I did that every day until right now, did you? You should know that there's nothing so crafty as a cat. After the relaxing clawing session I did indeed curl up on my comfy cushion on the sofa and soon dozed off.

Probably a couple of hours later, I heard the door open and Del came in. I wonder if he's got any treats in his pocket? I thought, so I jumped up and greeted him with a welcoming and encouraging purr. It worked – I knew he'd be a pushover – and he bent down, stroked me and gave me a lovely pink, juicy shrimp. Yummy! While I returned to my cushion, still savouring the taste, he went about his duties replacing the towels (ha ha!) and face cloths, then turning down the bedsheets and putting Sheila's favourite treats on the pillow; two chocolates. Then he gave me a final pat on the head and went off to carry on with his work. Sheila always says the room stewards and all the guys on this ship – who clean, cook and work in the bars and restaurants – do a wonderful job and she can't praise them enough. Well, I've noticed that everything is so shiny and bright and clean that unfortunately there's never any chance of the odd spider lurking in a dusty corner for me to catch.

Soon Sheila returned and was giggling to herself. What had happened now? I wondered.

"Well Misty," she said, "I've just had a dinner experience that was so awful it was really funny." Surely not, I thought, she always says how marvellous the food and service is on here. As if reading my mind she continued, "No, nothing wrong with the food, it was just the people on my table. Ha Ha!" It turned out that she had been put on a table with several other people, all singles like her. Well, that must have been good, I thought – you never know, even at her age, there must be a 'Mr Right' somewhere, and why not on this ship? Anyway, interspersed (yes, that's a good word I've picked up from your language!) with giggles she said that there were two elderly men, one very tall and very thin, one very short and very fat, and three equally elderly old ladies, two from overseas somewhere and the third was from up north in England. She, said Sheila, had dyed bright pink hair and was wearing a big red bow in it. Not quite the look Sheila would have adopted, I thought. As they all arrived at the table, the waiter introduced them and handed them the menus to look at. Sheila, who could talk the hind leg off a donkey – one of your quaint human expressions – was about to politely say good evening to start the conversation going, but on looking at them changed her mind. Not one of the other people said a word of greeting to anyone. All, without exception, sat there with pursed lips and po-faces. Nobody looked at each other and nobody uttered a single word. So Sheila buttoned it as well, as she didn't particularly fancy a conversation with them anyway. About a quarter of an hour later the starters arrived (first night on any ship is always a bit disorganised with slight delays at dinner as some people don't turn up as they are tired after journeying to the ship, or are still unpacking or whatever, others arrive but don't know which table they are at. By the second night all is under control again). Everyone ate their starters, still not a word was spoken. Next the soup and salad course was served. Still no talking! One of the elderly ladies went out (to try out the dastardly ship's water boxes) and didn't come back for ages so all the rest had to wait because due to 'eti-cat' the waiter had to wait until everyone had finished their course before he could serve the next. The main course arrived. Still not a word had been spoken. One of the foreign ladies ate so slowly, Sheila thought bedtime would have arrived before she finished. Still no talking! As by now it was well after 10.00 p.m. she couldn't stand it any longer so said she was sorry but time was getting on and she had to meet some people so she wouldn't stay for dessert. With an understanding smile from the waiter, she went to see the manager, whom she knew, and said don't dare put her on that table from hell again. Please swap to another. When she told him why, he also had to laugh and said he'd fix it for her to sit at a table with some nice people from then on. And he did and they were!.

After Sheila had gone into the non-bathroom and I'd cringed as I heard the thunderous roar of the water box, she said, "Come on Misty, we'll just go to the Café B for a coffee," (well you might want one, dear, I certainly don't) "and we won't be too late tonight because we've had a long day." Too right, I thought. I didn't really fancy moving to be honest so with a sigh of resignation I got up and let her put the lead on and we went along the, by now very familiar, passageway. Arriving at the luxurious coffee lounge, Sheila soon found a little table, hooked my lead round one of its legs, sat down and I – knowing the routine I had to follow by now – curled up underneath it. I had a good view of people's legs as they passed but not a lot else.

I heard Sheila chatting with some guy who seemed to work there and soon he bent down and said, "Hi, Misty, my name's Hanns, you're SO pretty! I've read your book, so you're clever too." Well, and don't I know it, I thought, and it was nice of him to agree with me. So I switched to purr mode and he smoothed my head and gave me a nice tickle behind the ears. Oh, he's definitely a cat lover, I thought, and as his next words were that he was soon going to buy a cat for his dear mother, I was proved right! Well, I'm a cat – of course, I'm always right!

Hanns went off to return a few minutes later with a glass of that sickly, hot frothy drink which he'd made even more sickly by adding some of Sheila's favourite naughty drink to it; Amoretto.

"Well," laughed Sheila, "I wonder how you remembered what I wanted before I even ordered it!" And they both burst into peals of hyena laughter.

A few minutes on and two pairs of ankles stopped at the table, one female with nice shoes, though not towering nearly as high as Sue's, and one with a much bigger pair which looked like brown suede boats to me. Sheila got up and they greeted each other like long lost friends. It seemed they had met many times on this ship before but Sheila had no idea they would be here on this trip.

"We've done a back-to-back," said the lady, "been to the Med and we're staying on now for the Canaries."

What on earth is she talking about? I thought, a back-to-back? Have they been somewhere walking around strapped together, one going forward and the other going backward? I shook my head, some other strange human custom I suppose. Each to his own!

"Yes," said her husband, "we had beautiful weather but the forecast for the next two days doesn't look good I'm afraid!" Oh dear, I thought, don't tell me I won't be able to sunbathe on the balcony! I emerged from under the table and Sheila introduced me to her friends.

"Oh," said the lady, "how nice to meet you, Misty, we've read your book and so has our daughter, she just loves cats." This is getting good, I thought, here we are only on the first night and everybody we meet seems to love cats! Purr mode switched on again, they both gave me a pat before telling Sheila that they'd all meet up again soon. What a pleasant couple, I thought, but again, although they spoke English, they sounded different from Sheila and our Cornish neighbours. They had a nice quiet sing-song sort of accent. I found it soothing. We cats have much the same accent anywhere (except our Oriental cousins) but it is certainly different with you humans. Sheila said their names were Mavis and Peter and they lived in Wales so I looked forward to when we would meet again. Also Hanns, he was nice too. He definitely didn't come from England as he had a different way of talking altogether, though he spoke perfect English. I wondered why he was called Hanns, but that was certainly a lot better than being called Feet I suppose!

Sheila finished her drink, unhooked the lead, waved goodbye to Hanns and off we went back to the stateroom for our 'early night', although it was already much later than when we usually go to bed at home.

DAY 2

I awoke suddenly, very, very early in the morning. Something felt a bit odd. The room, which had been just like any other room up until now, seemed to be moving a bit … or was I still dreaming? I sat up and looked around. Yes, one minute the floor seemed flat and the next it seemed to be on a slant. This kept happening – weird! In its way, it felt as if you were being gently rocked to sleep, so it wasn't an unpleasant sensation, just odd. I lay down again but stayed alert. Actually, the rocking feeling was nice so it wasn't long before I dozed off again. But suddenly an almighty jolt woke me up with a start. My bed seemed to be sliding towards the opposite side of the stateroom, so I leapt up and sprang right on top of Sheila who was, unbelievably, still sleeping. "What the..." she said, sitting up and uttering a word that an innocent little cat like me does NOT wish to hear! (Though I have to admit that I have uttered quite a few naughty cat words in my time, like when I have just missed a tasty spider which has annoyingly eluded my reach!).

"Don't you dare jump on me like that, Misty! And keep your claws in." Alright, keep your fur on, dear, I only wanted to let you know that something is not right here.

I got down on to the floor again but as I did so, there was another jolt and I slid over to join my bed which was now jammed against the sofa. "Oh dear," said Sheila, "sorry, Misty, I'm afraid we must have started to go through the Bay of Biscay towards The Azores. They did warn us that it might be rough as there is an exceptional, and unusually bad, tail end of a tornado approaching the UK." I sat and tried to decipher what she was talking about. It sounded like she said we were going through a bay of biscuits (cookies to you Amerrycan readers!) and what's a torn Ado? I guessed an 'Ado' could be some sort of animal as it seems to have a tail, but how on earth did it get itself torn? Maybe some other animal with sharp teeth gave it a going over? This was all too much for me – I have enough to take in with all the new sights I'm seeing on a ship, I can do without all these other odd human phrases to contend with as well! Still, let's stay with the moment, I thought, and hope the stateroom just keeps rocking smoothly and doesn't turn upside down!

Sheila got up and, staggering slightly, (she didn't have that many Amorettos last night did she?) went across and picked up my bed and put it back where it had been.

"Oh well, this'll be a bit of fun," she said, "makes it all the more exciting but I daresay a lot of the other passengers won't think that! Go back to bed, Misty, it's not 6.00 a.m. yet, just hang on tight and go to sleep again." Easier said than done, I thought, getting a little worried now as to what was going to happen. Still, she made her way back to her own bed, and I snuggled down again with claws in the 'ready to grip' position if another jolt came along. We slept for another hour or so and then a mighty jolt woke us both up and me and my bed slid over to the sofa again.

Sheila got up and gave me a comforting pat saying that I shouldn't worry, she'd been through rougher seas than this, it wouldn't be too long until we got through the storm and then things would be calm again. Let's hope so, I thought. She opened the glass door to the balcony a few inches and I nipped out to do my morning ablutions while she went into the non-bathroom and attended to her own. At least my litter box and other stuff had remained intact, wedged into the balcony's sheltered inner corner, but the floor outside was also heaving from side to side. I crept very slowly forward to have a peep through the glass wall at the sea below but the very big waves looked really scary so I quickly scurried back inside. Sheila then came out and cleared the litter box. Good girl, she never forgets her cat care duties! She then gave me my breakfast crunchies and while I ate them she got herself ready for the day, fussed about her head fur (sorry, hair!) and told me she was off for her own breakfast now and would collect me later for a wander around the ship. What new delights would I see today? I wondered, nothing outside I hoped. I went into the non-bathroom myself and had a nice claw stretch on the towel on the lower rail, then it was back to bed for a whisker clean, relaxing stretch and to doze off again. I was getting used to the constant rocking motion now, and it felt quite pleasant despite the odd really big jolt.

A while later Del came in. "Ello, Mistee," he said giving me a pat, "Eet's a bit choppy out there, don't go out onto the balcony. No sitting in the sun for you today." You're so right, Del! NO way! "E'res teetbit for you," he continued, giving me a tasty shrimp, "enjoy and I will do my work here." And he went around tidying up the non-bathroom, replacing the towels (as I'd hoped, he never noticed how one was now looking a bit threadbare!). I savoured the shrimp and then just sat and idly watched him, until he switched on a noisy carpet cleaning machine like the one Sheila uses at home, which is also a thing that scares me (don't forget that I am a wimp!). So I speedily retreated under the bed thinking he wouldn't reach me there, but he said, "Don't worry, Mistee, it won't hurt you!" and he DID sweep it under the bed although, as I had hidden behind the cases stored there, it didn't get me. Oh dear, I thought, I suppose he'll do that every day here – at least Sheila only does it once a week back home and I don't remember her ever using it under her bed! Anyway, I would be prepared when he came in with it again. His work done, Del went off and not long after Sheila returned.

"Well, things look nice in here" she remarked, "I hope you didn't get in Del's way and hold him up." No, I didn't. "Right, let's go," she said. She picked out a nautical style collar for me, with a little anchor hanging from it, put it on me, clipped on the dreaded lead and we started our wandering.

For some reason, Sheila didn't seem to be able to walk in a straight line along the slightly rocking passageway. She was zigzagging from side to side all the way. Don't know why, but I noticed that other people too were walking in this strange fashion, with a lot of laughing as sometimes they bumped into each other or the hand rails at the side of the passage. Well, I have four legs and am sited much nearer to ground level so there was no difficulty for me. But it took us twice as long as usual to arrive at the elevators. The unseen lady announced that we were arriving at Deck 4 so off we got and I saw a line of shops that looked ready to welcome Sheila and her wallet.

Several people were wandering around the shops which were filled with lots of tempting things for you humans, but nothing that would appeal to cats. There were all sorts of clothes, sparkly decorations for your wrists, ears and necks, handbags, cuddly toys, sweets and chocolates, bottles of that sickly stuff you drink and too many other things to mention. I had the usual comments made to me and lots of pats and we met some more friends of Sheila's, called Mary and Eric, who I had met too when I was on the ship last year. Mary, like Sheila, seemed to be enjoying the shopping thing but Eric, like me really, didn't look very keen. Sheila agreed to meet up with them later and we carried on. Goodness, me she seems to know so many people on this ship, I thought, no wonder she always refers to it as her second home!

Sheila picked up a cuddly teddy bear wearing a tee shirt with the name of the ship on the front. Oh dear, I thought, not another one! Half our house is filled up with teddy bears she has brought home as souvenirs of her travels. She seems to be compelled to get one from every country she has visited and from the various ships she's been on (and that's a hell of a lot in over 20 years of cruising!). I scowled up at her. But surprisingly she replaced it on the shelf. "Yes I know, Misty" she said glancing down at me, "I was only looking. I'll resist him because I've three or four from this ship already but I'm afraid I WILL be getting a few more small ones on this trip because, strangely enough, I've never got one from Madeira or anywhere in the Canaries. So we left the shops without her buying anything – that's a first I thought – But then I remembered, there were another 13 days to go yet!

We headed off to the elevators again but this time took one from a group that were near to the bow of the ship, whereas our normal ones were at the stern end. I wondered why. We got out at a higher deck this time, Deck 14, and Sheila led me in the direction of a huge lounge with one of those naughty cocktail bars in it and a circular centre wooden floor with a raised platform behind it. I wondered what it was. But the thing that really caught my eye was that the whole of this huge, huge area was surrounded with glass windows and the view all round was amazing. Water, water everywhere. If I had seen this on my first visit last year, when I was nervous, I reckon I would have passed out but now, as I said earlier, I was confident and, even though it looked pretty terrifying at this particular moment with all the huge waves breaking all around us, I wasn't scared, just awestruck! This room was rocking about even more than our stateroom, but being up at the front here I guessed we were heading smack right into the waves. There were already quite a lot of people sitting in groups and Sheila went up to four people who, it turned out, she had met earlier and joined them.

"Here's Misty!" she said and they said the usual stuff and I got four nice pats, "but I'm not sure she'll be much of a help to us," she continued, causing them all to turn on the hyena laughs. "Misty, these are Steve and Alison, and Steve and Linda, and we're going to show you how clever we are." More hyena laughs. She sat down and I curled up at her feet. What were they going to do now? I wondered.

Soon a young girl with fair hair, and petite like me, arrived at the central wooden floor and told everyone to come up and collect paper and pencils. "I'll go," said Sheila, "It's Sam, I must go and say hello. She also lives in Cornwall like us." Funny, I thought, I've never seen her before … but I suppose there are a lot of people living in Cornwall, apart from us and the neighbours. Sheila returned and the jolly atmosphere in the room suddenly changed slightly and everyone was now looking challengingly at each other.

"Now," said Sam "remember, folks, this is just a game so enjoy. Give all your teams a name and then we'll start." The two Steves, Alison, Linda and Sheila decided that our team should be called 'Sea Legs', though I would have preferred 'Sea Paws' myself! Sam then started asking all sorts of questions and there were some discussions amongst the members of the various teams, not less ours, before they wrote down their answers, but I really didn't know what they were doing so lost all interest and drifted off into sleep mode again. I only awoke when I heard Sheila and her new friends clapping their hands and laughing amongst themselves. It seemed they were third on the score board out of the whole roomful of groups. They agreed to meet up to carry on the questions (progressive trivia they called it) on the next day at sea and we said our goodbyes and headed off to the elevators again.

This time we went lower than I'd been before … to Deck 3. Sheila led me over to an area with stands containing papers and stuff and stopped by one. I looked up expectantly but there was nothing that would interest me on it. She took a couple of sheets and then moved to another and picked up a daily paper muttering that she didn't know why she bothered to get it, it only contained bad news. Still, I could see a lot of people lounging about nearby on those comfy leather sofas that seem to grow on this ship like a forest, and they all seemed to be reading daily papers though, with my sharp eyes, I could see that they weren't all in English, but in strange languages as well.

"Right," said Sheila, "we'll walk to the other end and get the elevator back to the stateroom and then I want to go to the Spa and gym to fix a hair appointment. She gave a wry grin, "and don't expect to see ME in action in the gym, Misty!" Well I gathered that dear, the only exercise YOU take is walking round shops. I like to keep fit myself so maybe I could have a go on something if elf and safety would allow it.

We strolled along Deck 3 and passed a bar where there were two giant TV screens on the walls with groups of men watching other men chasing or kicking a ball about. Purrsonally, I would have been more interested in watching them kicking mice or birds about but that, I've grown to realise, is just a fantasy that we cats have. As we got nearer the middle where the passageway opened out into a large open space I could see a crowd of people all watching a man in a white coat and wearing a tall white hat who was talking to them. Suddenly, I sniffed. Was that fish I could smell? Yes, FISH! As we approached the people surrounding him, sure enough he was holding a big salmon (about three times the length of me!) and he seemed to be demonstrating how to cut it into pieces. This looks promising, I thought. Maybe if I ask nicely, he'll give me a piece! But Sheila, sensing my thoughts, kept a tight grip on the lead so no chance there. We stopped to watch what he was doing and Sheila whispered to me that they did all sorts of demonstrations and held culinary classes on this ship, as it was so renowned for its excellent food, showing people how to do the same in their own homes. Huh, something that YOU'LL never achieve I thought. If you can't do something in the microwave in five minutes you don't want to know! A few minutes later the crowd broke up and the man started packing up his gear.

"Hi, Darran," said Sheila, "so that's how it's done, eh?" He smiled at her and said he remembered her from her last cruise. "Well," replied Sheila, "I have something for you that I will get the other Darren (Darren with an 'e') to pass on. It's a recipe book describing the meals served at Captains' Tables on the ocean going cruise liners of the twenties and thirties – I saw it and thought of you!"

"Oh, thanks," he said," that sounds intriguing – I look forward to seeing it." We carried on and I thought, Sheila has some cheek hasn't she? Nothing like coming on a cruise and giving the executive chef a recipe book!

Back in the stateroom, Sheila let me out on the balcony which was still heaving about – it hadn't been so noticeable when we'd been lower down on Deck 3 as it was up here. I did what was required, she tidied up after and then, just as we were about to leave, Sheila noticed a red light blinking on the little machine you speak into. It turned out it was a message for us to meet up with China boy, Peng Fei, in the afternoon. That's nice, I thought. I like him. He gave me a ball last time, I wonder if he'll give me anything this time? A few minutes later we were on our way to the spa area, which was only one deck up. So, we walked up the stairs instead of using the elevator. Well, I guess she can manage ONE flight of stairs without puffing!

One deck up and the swaying motion was worse than ever. No great problem for little me but Sheila was back in zigzag mode again, as were several other people we passed en route. We arrived at the Spa, a huge place looking very glamorous and with all sorts of rooms leading off the main reception area. People were walking (zigzagging!) about and lots were wearing fluffy white toweling coats like the one I'd noticed hanging on the back of our stateroom's non-bathroom door, but alas too high up for me to reach. Have they only just got out of bed? I wondered. We approached a desk with two young lady humans sitting behind it and Sheila arranged an appointment with the furdresser (no, hairdresser!) for the next week in time for the last formal night.

Then we carried on until we came to the gym. It was full of those strange walking pavement machines. Also lots of those two wheeled contraptions you like to ride and which seem an utter waste of time to me as when I was here last time, despite how hard the people pedaled on them, they never got them to move forward. There were also lots of other machines with bars and weights dangling from them that I didn't really understand. However, despite all these delights there weren't very many people using them and the guy in charge, Tim, was looking rather bored. We went over to him; he patted me and said he'd heard there was a famous cat on board. He got an appreciative purr for that! Then he said the ship swaying was the reason not many people were there. I could see two or three hardy souls pedaling furiously but nobody else. Listening to him and Sheila chatting it seemed that never had they had such a bad spell of weather in the Bay of Biscuits as this. It was most unusual. Sheila said that she had had an email from some cruising friends, Connie and Ron, who live in Jersey (excuse me, but how can you live in a jersey?) and they had said that all the ferries across to them had been stopped because of this tail end of the torn Ado. Even Force 10 gales we sometimes get on this route would normally have no effect on this ship he told Sheila, but this is exceptionally bad but, there again, he shrugged, the weather worldwide is doing weird things nowadays.

"Now," said Sheila, "as it's so quiet here do you think Misty could have a go on the treadmill? I think she'd love it.

"Yeah, why not," he said smiling, "she'll have fun."

So we walked over to one of the moving pavement machines. He hooked my lead around the control unit at the front and I hopped on to the platform. Well, what am I supposed to do now? I thought, looking up at him expectantly. Do I start walking? Suddenly the platform started moving backward – goodness, I went into fast walk mode and weirdly, although I was using all four legs, I didn't move forward and it took quite a lot of effort just to keep in the same place. This is certainly something cats would never waste energy on, walking but not moving anywhere. It's pretty pointless really when you think of it, but I can see why you humans who need the exercise would like it. There was no chance to stop or slow down as the platform kept moving. I could see Sheila and Tim laughing at me. That put a scowl on my face, and I started running … I'll show them, I thought!

"Get your camera ready," I heard Tim say to Sheila, and then the platform speeded right up. I was thrown backwards and really had to step on it to keep (a) upright and (b) stay on the platform at all. Shrieks of laughter from the pair of them now … the platform got even faster and all of a sudden I was flying backwards but just managed to dig my claws in to avoid being literally thrown off altogether. Then, mercifully, the platform slowed down and Tim picked me up and gave me a cuddle.

"Well, Misty," he smiled, "you DID want to try it!" Sheila by this time was crying with laughter but eventually pulled herself together, said goodbye and thanked Tim and then we left. I don't know why she thanked him for making a fool of me(!) but I had to admit that I did actually enjoy the ride. But now all I fancied was some lunch and when we got back to the stateroom I tucked gratefully into some prawn flavoured crunchies and Sheila went off to get her own food. I got myself comfy on my cushion and soon nodded off. Well, after my exertions in the gym that wasn't surprising I suppose! The swaying motion didn't seem so bad now so maybe things were returning to normal in the notorious bay.

Some while later, Sheila appeared and she changed her top, fussed around with her hair, put another collar on me and off we set to meet Peng Fei. Apparently, Sheila usually met him in the buffet but as I was not allowed in there, it was back to the coffee lounge again. It was very full when we arrived as it is a popular place, particularly mid-afternoon and mid-morning, and as nobody was outside on the decks today, it was even more crowded than usual. I couldn't see Hanns around but suddenly another guy with a huge smile on his face came up to us and it was obviously someone else that Sheila knew.

"Hi, Randy," she smiled, "good to see you again. Do you think you can find us a seat somewhere, we're meeting Peng Fei in a minute."

"Of course," he said, and led us to a table in a corner. They chatted for a few moments and then he had to dash off to fetch drinks for other people but said he'd be back as soon as he saw Peng Fei had arrived. I settled down under the table and began ankle watching again. Not long after, Peng Fei arrived and bent down to give me a nice pat and a tickle under the chin before he sat down opposite Sheila. Randy appeared with two big glasses of that hot, frothy coffee for them, plus some naughty, sickly looking cakes, and I dozed off again as I knew Sheila and Peng would be catching up on their news and chattering to each other non-stop. I don't know why you humans talk so much; we animals don't waste our breath saying words that aren't needed. We get our messages across in just a few miaows or barks as the case may be. Anyway, I switched to sleep mode and let them get on with it.

I felt a tug on my collar and woke up to see that Sheila and Peng Fei were getting ready to leave. He was saying that he feared the big show would have to be postponed because it seemed that, while for the past few hours it had felt calmer in the eye of the torn Ado, now we were going out of it through the other side, so Sue was going to wait until 5.00 p.m. to decide whether the show could go on. If not, and the weather wasn't better tomorrow either, it would have to be cancelled completely which was a great shame because it was the biggest and most spectacular of all the shows on this ship, but there were other shows booked in for all the other evenings to come.

I listened with interest because now I realised that the torn Ado had an eye as well as a tail – just one eye? Sounds a bit like an alien to me, I shivered, I don't think I'd like to meet it!

"See you in a few days then," smiled Peng and he walked away. We went back to the stateroom and yes, it did seem to be swaying quite a bit more now. Oh dear!

Sheila switched on the TV on the wall and I settled down on my cushion for a while. "Well, Misty," she said, "it seems the wind is going to be very strong again overnight and it says that it is very bad where we live in Cornwall too. Never mind, only a day and we will have passed through it and be in The Azores and it'll be nice again."

Well, bring it on, I thought. A little later I could hear her on the talking machine ordering my dinner, and then she started getting herself dolled up to go for a naughty cock's tail – or whatever they're called – before her own meal. I nipped outside and, afterwards, Sheila brought in my stuff as she said we'd better be safe than sorry when it got rough out there. So she stowed it away temporarily in the non-bathroom while I ate my delicious meal of venison pate followed by halibut chunks in sauce. Delightful! I retired to my bed, cleaned whiskers and fell asleep so I never heard her leave. Sometime later I awoke with a start and realised that, once again, me and my bed were making a trip to the other side of the stateroom and we landed up against the sofa with a bump. Oh well, I thought, we seem wedged here now so hopefully we won't shift anymore. I looked around but nothing else seemed to have moved, even the bottle of bubbly in its bucket of ice on the low table. When Del came in to carry out his night time duties (and those included, of course, giving me a shrimp!) he did seem to be a bit slower than he had been yesterday as even he didn't seem to be able to walk in a straight line tonight. Once he'd gone, it was into the non-bathroom for a good old claw stretch on the towel and back to bed. But it was difficult to get to sleep. I could hear knocking sounds and the whooshing of the wind outside. They were right about the weather, things didn't look good.

Eventually, Sheila returned and asked if I was OK? Course I am, dear, I'm not always a scaredy cat and a bit of wind wasn't going to frighten me!

"Well, I'm only going to have a nightcap coffee now," she said, "the show was cancelled I'm afraid, so I didn't see Peng Fei perform, but there was another singer who stepped in to take over and she was very good. Come on, let's go – it's only 11.30, the night is young still." At home we would have been tucked up in bed by 10.30 p.m. I thought, how she changes when on this ship!

We got to the elevator taking twice the time we should have because of Sheila walking twice the distance. Eventually, we reached the coffee lounge and she didn't even have to order her disgusting frothy and Amoretto mix because Hanns had already seen us coming and, as we arrived at a handy table, he put the glass down with a flourish. There certainly weren't so many people around now, I thought, watching a few zigzagging past us. Sheila echoed my thoughts because she was telling Hanns that there were a lot of people missing at dinner and even the theatre wasn't full. They were probably seasick she was saying, something that had never troubled her, or me come to that. Nearly an hour (and two Amoretto concoctions later) we made our way back and this time it took even longer to get home. Eventually Sheila got herself to bed, not without a few of those naughty words as she swayed around the room, not due to the two Amorettos I say in her defence, but due to the ever increasing rocking motion. I settled down in my little bed – safely jammed between the sofa and the low table – and pondered over the day's events. I must apologise to you people reading this as I think I have probably rambled on a bit too much, but this has been the beginning of the cruise and so there have been people to meet and catch up with, and things to see and for me to describe. After the next sea day tomorrow I shall be much more brief, as I don't want you all to fall asleep before you get to the end of my little book. Sorry!

Some hours later, I awoke to feel that the movement of the ship was much more intense. It must have been around dawn as I could see a slight chink of daylight showing through the curtains at the balcony door. Sheila must have woken up too because she also suddenly sat up in bed. Suddenly, we both glanced at the low table and the bottle in its bucket which was now almost full to the brim with water slopping about. The ice had melted overnight and would be replaced with fresh ice by Del in the morning. Because it would take Sheila three or four days to drink it all, he had done the old trick of sticking a teaspoon in the neck of the bottle. Somehow, this stops it going flat he said. But of course this meant that with no cork fitted tightly into the bottle, if it fell over all the liquid would spill out. As we both watched, there was a very big jolt and the

46

bucket started to slide along the table.

"OMG," said Sheila, "it's all going to fall off the end of the table and swamp everything. That mustn't happen – I'll have to ditch it." She got out of bed, stumbled towards the table and lifted off the bucket and bottle. "Blimey, that's heavy," she squawked and tried to get across to the non-bathroom as quickly as she could but she was literally swaying from one side of the room to the other all the way so I thought she'd fall over herself at any minute. That would have been something worth putting into a TV programme she likes to watch where people, and even cats and dogs, are shown in embarrassing and funny situations. But she finally made it to the non-bathroom and I heard her tipping the lot down the sink. "Phew," she said coming out with the now empty bucket, "that was a near thing! If it had fallen off it would have ruined the carpet and half drowned you into the bargain!"

Well, blow the carpet, I thought, she seems more concerned about that than me! I felt a sulk coming on …

"Still," she continued, "I had a glass out of it when we left and I'm not fussed about drinking any more really, so I tipped the rest away and shoved the bottle in the bin. Del will probably think I came home last night and drunk the entire remainder of the bottle and got totally bladdered," she laughed.

Sheila got into her bed, and I curled up and both of us tried to go to sleep again. Easier said than done as the knocking noises and roaring of the wind didn't help. Still, apart from disaster with the bottle of bubbly, when we did get up later at breakfast time, nothing else in the stateroom or the non-bathroom seemed to have moved at all. It was still pretty rocky but by the next evening things were looking much more promising, though sadly still not good enough for the big show to be put on.

DAY 3

Well, just one more day on the water and I would get to see an azore! I couldn't wait. And also it would be rather nice to put my paws on solid ground again. This past couple of days had been something of a strange experience for me with all the rolling and swaying about, quite fun really, and Sheila always says if it's choppy outside it livens things up a bit, but lots of the other passengers had not been best pleased – as if it was the ship's fault! But people, nobody – human or animal or bird – is stronger than Mother Nature. So, no point in grumbling about it. They should have taken themselves off to one of the bars and drowned their sorrows in one of those sickly drinks. Though, on second thoughts, if they had been feeling seasick already that might have made them even worse. Ha Ha! Miaow! Miaow!

When we got up, Sheila managed to get the litter box outside again so I could attend to my morning ablutions before she gave me my breakfast of tasty crunchies and went off to get her own morning delights up in the buffet as usual.

After my breakfast, I thought I might go outside, but there was no handy gap (which was usually left for me between the glass doors) so that knocked that idea on the head. But I could still hear the wind whooshing outside so I suppose that was why. I wished the silly torn Ado would hurry up and go on its way and leave us behind. Not in the best of moods, I gave the towel a good going over and retreated back to bed again. Shortly after, in came Del with a big smile on his face and presented me with a very large shrimp, almost a baby lobster.

"Ello, Mistee," he said, "You 'ave to be very good today because the housekeeper is coming specially to see us to make sure we 'ave done everything right, as I've never had to look after a cat guest before! We 'ave to make sure we follow all the rules." Those elf and safety guys again, I thought! Well, last time I passed with flying colours and Sheila and Del were both very fussy so I'm sure all would be OK. NOW I realised that the giant shrimp was a bribe. Whatever, it was a treat to eat and my mood immediately brightened.

Del went about his usual tasks and I retreated under the bed when he brandished that noisy carpet cleaning machine about. I was under there still when he brought out the towels from the non-bathroom. This was lucky because he suddenly noticed all the frayed bits on the end of one of them. "That's bad," I heard him mutter, "must have got ripped in the washing machine, I wonder how nobody noticed it. I will have to report it – this is just not up to the standard we expect on this ship." Phew, I'm sure I would have looked guilty if I had been in front of him, I would have to be more careful in future and disguise my efforts better.

Casually, I strolled out from under the bed and was just about to jump onto my cushion when there was a loud knock on the door and a voice said, "Housekeeping here!"

"Now, sit still Mistee – on the floor in the corner," said Del as he rushed to open the door. In strode a very important looking lady wearing one of those smart navy coats with gold rings on the sleeves and carrying a large board with a paper clipped to it. She looked rather scary...

"Good morning, Del" she said, "I understand we have a feline on this trip?"

"Yes," said Del, pointing at me, "she has been on here before and is very well-behaved and clean in her habits."

"OK, we'll see," said the lady, and started to walk around the stateroom noting things down on her clipboard as she did. She then opened the door and went on to the balcony. Del was looking nervous but I wasn't. She was beginning to get my back up ... I bet I'm fussier than SHE is, I thought. Eventually, she came back in, her immaculate hair looking a bit tussled from the wind. "Well, everything out there seems shipshape," she said, "in fact everything here has scored ten out of ten – there's only one thing more I have to do and that's make sure she doesn't have any fleas." Fleas? FLEAS? ME? How dare she, I've NEVER had fleas. I am brushed every couple of days and Sheila puts drops into my neck every few weeks. "Now, Del," said the lady, "has she a comb somewhere? Get it for me please and I will run it through her fur." No, you damn well will NOT ... and before either of them could grab me, I was under the bed again.

We then spent the next quarter of an hour playing hide and seek. Needless to say, I won! Del tried to bribe me to come out with another (smaller) shrimp and the scary lady was tapping her foot on his newly cleaned carpet as he did so.

"It's no good," he was saying to her when suddenly the door opened and Sheila came in.

"What on earth's happening here?" she said when she saw

Del on his knees and the head housekeeper watching him with a peeved expression on her face.

"It's Mistee's elf and safety inspection, Mees Sheila," spluttered Del, "and she won't let my boss look at her fleas."

"Fleas?" echoed Sheila, "she hasn't got any. I'll show you, don't worry yourself. Misty, come here immediately please!" I knew that tone of voice which she doesn't have to use often – her 'SHE who must be obeyed' voice – so I thought I'd better do as she said. I came straight out and went to Sheila's feet, sat down and stared up at her. Let the lady officer see just how well trained I was … when I wanted to be. Ha Ha! Miaow! Miaow! Sheila put one of the dirty towels on the low table (thankfully not the mutilated one) and told me to sit on it and then lie down. I followed her instructions to the letter and out of the corner of my eye I could see that madam housekeeping was looking impressed. "Please do come up close and look," Sheila said to her, and when she did so, ran the comb through all my fur proving that there were no fleas anywhere. The lady put another tick on her clipboard sheet and at last cracked her face with a smile.

"I'm sorry," she said, "I had to be official in all this. I was told by our hotel director that Misty has indeed been on here before and is an honoured guest of the ship – and even an author (a puzzled look came over her face) but I didn't really believe him. And, of course," looking at Sheila, "you will know how strict the Health and Safety people are." Sheila nodded. "Anyway," she continued, "everything is absolutely fine and I'm pleased to have met Misty in person." She gave me a pat on the head.

"Well, thank you," said Sheila, "I will ensure that we don't break any rules." Then she took rather a gamble, I thought, and cheekily gave the housekeeper the details of my first book in case she wanted to read it.

Once she had gone, Del breathed a sigh of relief, gathered up the towels and left. Sheila said she was going to the next session of the progressive trivia but didn't think I would particularly want to go so would collect me after. But I pawed at the lead as now I had started my new hobby of ankle watching, there would be a lot there for me to inspect so I DID want to go along. "Oh, come on then or I'll be late," she said, "I've had enough drama for one morning with your fleas – or lack of them," she quickly added as she saw my expression change from happy to furious. Lead clipped on, we hurried up to the big observation lounge above.

As before, there were many teams all chattering and laughing and it was pretty noisy. Sheila joined the other Sea Legs and I settled at her feet and surveyed the ankles passing by … all shapes and sizes, I could almost write a book about them, I thought! Sheila was talking with two of her companions, Steve and Linda I think it was, but there again it could have been Steve and Alison, and they were keen walkers and liked to keep themselves fit. Pity Sheila wasn't the same! They walked round the ship every day counting their steps on little machines strapped to their wrists called pedometers and had a kind of competition between each other as to who took the most steps in a day. Sounds interesting, I mewsed. Then I heard them saying that Misty should do that too and have a competition with the captain's dog as they had heard he had one that he adored. What? A dog is on board? No way!

"Well," said Sheila, "I personally know the Captain who has a lovely dog, an Akita called Pasa, but he is on leave this trip. So don't worry, Misty, there's no dog on board." Thank the lord for that, I thought. They all laughed.

"Well," said Steve, "Misty and Pasa could have worn pawometers on their legs (more laughter) and Misty would have won hands down (paws down!) because she would have taken about six steps to Pasa's one." They were still laughing when petite Sam arrived and they all got serious again as the questions commenced. There weren't any ankles passing by now so I dozed off. At the end of the questions it seemed Sea Legs were still up there near the top of the leaderboard, so everyone went their different ways looking pleased with themselves. We headed down to Deck 5 and the coffee lounge again.

We were just about to sit down when a voice said, "Hi, Misty. Are you coming to do some more exercising later?"

"Oh, it's you, Tim," said Sheila, "I didn't recognise you all smart in a shirt and tie, and what snazzy cufflinks you're wearing!" Oh dear, I recognised him now, it was the guy in the gym and NO, I am certainly NOT going to make a fool of myself on the moving pavement again just to amuse him and Sheila.

"I'm going to an important meeting shortly," said Tim, "so I couldn't just turn up in sports gear. Is it OK if I join you for a little while in the meantime?" Meantime? What's that? I know people can be mean – like my first owners – but time? Although, now I come to think of it, I have heard people say they've had a 'happy time'. Perhaps it can be mean as well. Another one of your strange human expressions! I sat down under the table to have a cat nap and Randy came over and brought their drinks and they chatted about this and that until Tim went off to his meeting.

"There's been a blow out $10 sale on Deck 4," said Sheila, "so we'll nip down there to see what they've got left before lunchtime, come on, wake up!" So I was dragged off to the shops in which I had no interest whatsoever ... I felt a sulk coming on.

Outside the row of shops on Deck 4 there were crowds of people, mainly females, all pushing and shoving to look at the bargains set out on long tables. It was a miracle I didn't get flattened! It's lucky we cats are alert to all movements at all angles around us so Tim needn't have joked about me taking exercise, I got plenty outside here jumping this away and that to avoid all the feet. Sheila eventually came away clutching several items, thankfully no teddy bears, paid for them and we went back to the stateroom again. It seemed like a haven of peace after all the rabble outside the shops. I went and sat expectantly looking up at the talking machine and Sheila took the hint so a few minutes later my lunch appeared. She went off to get hers and I jumped up on my cushion and switched to sleep mode.

The rest of the day passed much as the day before. After my dinner I just stayed in the stateroom relaxing whilst Sheila went to the theatre although, as I said earlier, the naughty torn Ado had still made it impossible for the main show to go on. After Del had paid his evening visit (and no he didn't see the results of my claw stretching today, I'd made sure of that!) I did think that the swaying motion of the ship seemed to be calming down a bit and yes, by the following morning all was calm again. When Sheila finally arrived back she said she had been to a late night game show called 'The Liars' Club' or sometimes 'Call My Bluff' which she said was really, really funny and a bit saucy too. What was she on about now? I thought, how can sauce be funny, it's just tasty, surely? Anyway, as long as she had enjoyed herself – so what! Come on dear, lights out … I'm ready for bed. So that was that, the end of the third day and tomorrow I would be treading on foreign soil and maybe even finding an azore hidden somewhere!

DAY 4

We awoke to bright sun and, at last, I was able to sit outside and have my breakfast whilst looking at the view. Mid-morning it was to the coffee lounge again and we got there quicker now that Sheila could walk in a straight line again. Randy came over with the frothy stuff and then Sheila's friend, Mary, came and joined us. It seemed she had also been at the saucy Liars' Club last night and the two of them were laughing together about it. I gathered petite Sam had hosted the show and Sue and two other guys were the liars. One was a dishy young man, the activity manager, called Maarten, that all the ladies in the audience seemed to fancy. Mary and Sheila were exclaiming about the very tight trousers he wore. Think they called them 'drainpipes'. That reminded me of one of your expressions I've heard before … like a rat up a drainpipe. Maybe the ladies in the audience watching Maarten would have liked to have run up his drainpipes.

After our coffee break, nothing much happened that you would be interested to read about and after lunch we finally arrived at The Azores. Sheila made sure she had my passport documents, and after we got off the ship I looked around me to see if I could spot an 'azore', but as I didn't know what one looked like, it was a futile task so I gave up. What I could see were lots and lots of boats all clustered together around the dockside and behind were rows of white houses and taller buildings and beyond all of them were hills … all this against a background of a blue sky looked pretty well purrfect to me. AND it was lovely and hot. We strolled along past some little shops and cafes and past the boats. I saw that several of them were taking people on whale watching trips. Aaah, so now I remembered Sheila's friends Mavis and Peter saying they lived in Whales – maybe they were out here to visit their family. I wouldn't have minded going on one of these trips, mind you, watching was as far as I would want to go with a whale, too near and it'd have me for a titbit. But it seemed we weren't going to whale watch, Sheila continued walking along by the sea. It felt really nice to get my paws on dry land again though. I could see that many of the passengers from the ship were strolling along too but there were also people who lived here I suppose and they spoke yet another language I'd never heard. Some of them had dogs with them, but most were small and some were carried about in their owner's handbags.

We did come across a lady with four little snappy, yappy Chihuahuas who threw themselves right at me. Oh yeah boys, think you can frighten me? Cats can run rings around dogs – wanna see? I leapt forward as far as the dreaded lead would allow me and spat right in the face of the leading one. Ha! Take that! That stopped it in its tracks but the other three leapt forward as far as their leads would allow. The woman holding them shouted something at us that didn't sound too polite and for good measure I gave them a hiss and a growl. This was getting to be fun. I may be frightened of big birds and BIG dogs but certainly not stupid little dogs. Several people stopped to watch, hoping for a fight, but once they had seen my claws come out, the dogs retreated whimpering and two of them even jumped up into the lady's arms. Sissies! Sheila grabbed me and picked me up too, spoil sport.

"Come on, for goodness sake, Misty," said Sheila, "Behave yourself! Don't taunt them any longer, you won the contest." Well, they started it all anyway, but yes I did, didn't I? A cat will win over a dog any time as I told you. She hurried on past the woman and the four dogs who were now yapping loud enough to wake the dead. Spotting a frothy coffee place with tables and chairs outside, she sat down placing me back on the ground again, but she firmly held her grip on the lead so there was no chance of another doggy encounter. Yes, I guess it was rather out of character for me to get into fighting mode but they just got my back up (literally!).

We sat there for a little while, Sheila enjoying her coffee and me enjoying the sun. In fact it was almost too hot for me and I wished I had a zip in my fur coat so I could have undone it. Some people from the ship passed by and stopped for a chat. It seemed they were soon going on a tour to see the famous lakes and pools in the island, but Sheila said that on this cruise she wouldn't be doing any island tours herself, because she had done them before, so would be just touring shops. Presently, we got up and continued walking along by the sea which was now so different from the way it had been over the past few days – smooth and glittering under the sunshine. Going closer to the edge I could even spot, with my sharp eyes, tiny little creatures swimming in it. Fishes and shrimps I expect, but no I wasn't going to get myself wet trying to catch any when I could get them brought to me on a plate whenever I wished. A couple of hours later we turned back and, arriving at the dockside again, Sheila dragged me around some of the shops. She appeared to be looking for a teddy bear but didn't get lucky … oh, what a shame! Miaow! Miaow!

Back on board it was time for food again – now I know why people on cruises constantly talk about the food, it seems to be available at any hour of the day and night. And, judging by the size of some of the people on this trip, they took full advantage of it. I settled down as usual whilst Sheila dolled herself up and went off for her naughty pre-dinner cocks' tails in the Passport Bar saying that she would collect me after dinner as she wasn't going to a show tonight but to the disco and casino. I'd been in the casino before but I wasn't sure what a disco was, but no doubt all would be revealed later. And it was! What a scary, noisy place! I didn't like it at all. I wanted to stick my paws into my ears. Now, I know that Sheila likes her music (pop music I think she calls it) and I have to endure listening to it on the music channel on the TV each night at home so she can keep up with her top twenty favourites, but it was never as loud at home as in this disco place. My ears are much sharper than yours, like my eyes, and so everything seemed at least three times as loud to me as to you. In fact, I often think that the young people of today who seem always to be walking around holding little machines with wires coming out of them into their ears must be deaf … yes, maybe that's it – discos are so loud because the young people in them are deaf! I cringed behind Sheila's legs and fortunately she got the message that I didn't like this place so we moved on to the casino.

I have to say I'm not keen on this place either as all the

machines seem to be playing different tunes at the same time, and at pretty high volume too. Still, I know madam likes going there and sometimes she gets lucky, so I just sat by her feet and resigned myself to it. When I'd first been here, last year, I heard her muttering to herself about not winning but at least getting her 'steak' back so she could use it again on the next night. It turned out not to be the steak I know and love though, just a slip of white paper. Boring, boring! Tonight much the same happened, no winnings but her 'steak' back. As she got up I heard the person on the next door machine say to his wife that he was going to the tables to buy some chips. Chips? I know Sheila gets them from time to time from our local fish and chip shop, and gives me a few bits of her fish and occasionally an odd piece of chip as a treat. But here in the casino? No, yet another disappointment – just a pile of round plastic circles. Well, I can't say that this evening had been exactly my favourite, but there's always tomorrow! Back to the coffee place for madam's nighttime Amoretto treat, then to the stateroom and bed!

DAY 5

One more day at sea and it was spent much as the others except that, because now it was lovely and sunny and the sea was calm later in the morning, we went out on deck. Up to Deck 14 and we walked along past a pool where there were loads of people stretched out on low lying chairs. Some looked very chic in those two-piece swimming outfits you ladies like to wear, and some ... er, didn't! Why is it that people of generous proportions on holiday seem to like to show off bits of their bodies that others would never normally see (or want to!) in garish coloured shorts and tops that at home they would never think of wearing. Maybe it's because none of their friends would see them. I know that Sheila would never show off her infamous thighs in shorts anywhere – she wouldn't want to frighten anyone. Sorry Sheila! Being a cat I am allowed to make catty comments. Perhaps the most weird sight I saw on that day was a plump, elderly lady human with a yellow straw hat, decorated with what looked like bunches of grapes, perched on top of long grey hair hanging right down to below her bottom (butt to you Ammerycans reading this!). She had on a scarlet bikini top that left nothing to the imagination and under this wore brightly striped pink, white and green harem pants coming down to just above her knees. This charming ensemble was completed by pale blue toe-less shoes and a multitude of gold chains round each wrist and ankle. Well, I would certainly recognize THOSE ankles if they passed me by again, but to be honest I hoped they wouldn't. Miaow! Miaow!

Passing by this apparition, we arrived at the far end of the pool and Sheila stopped at an area of flat water that had coloured dancing waterspouts shooting up from it. What fun – she let out the lead a bit and I flicked my paws at the water jets trying to catch one. I didn't and came away with wet feet but I had enjoyed this game when we were in here before and I'm glad Sheila remembered to stop. In fact she had spotted another couple of her friends, Val and Ken, and was chatting to them. Oh yes, I remembered them from my last trip. They had a grandson with them then and we had all played a game where we had to get small balls into holes. I won! They seemed to spend most of their time in the casino though, playing other games, and before we walked on Sheila said she might see them up there one evening later on. Throwing her steak away I suppose!

Next, we walked up some outside stairs and came to the best part of the outside of the ship for me – a lovely green real grass lawn. People were walking around it, or sitting at the edge of it and many were playing games on it – rolling big black balls towards a small white one, or hurling rings over sticks. There was also a bar and Sheila sat down in a wicker chair near it telling me to lie on the grass and enjoy a rollover ... which I did. A tall smiley bartender came up and, yes, yet again it was somebody from her 'floating family'. He was called Mircea and they spent a few moments catching up on their news before he came back with a bright orange coloured drink in a tall glass with an umbrella on the top of it. Funny, it wasn't raining was it? We sat there peacefully, Sheila drinking her cock's tail and me drinking in the sun and the happy atmosphere around us. My mind was working furiously, if I could somehow escape from the lead for a few moments I would just love to rescue the little white ball that was being bullied by the big black ones.

And then suddenly my chance arrived! When Mircea next passed by Sheila asked him if she could take his photo. "Of course," he smiled. Whilst she fumbled in her bag for her picture taking machine, she passed him my lead to hold but as he was about to take it I jerked it out of his hand and ran towards the little white ball. As I reached it, I pushed it away from the black balls clustered around it and, ignoring the startled shouts from the people playing the game, I then had a wonderful time patting it this way and that for a few minutes. Well, sorry folks for spoiling your game, but now it was MY time to play! Actually, they seemed more amewsed than angry and took out their own picture machines to take pictures of me.

"The people back home," I heard one guy say, "just won't believe that a cat suddenly turned up on a ship during our game of bowls!" Laughter all round.

Sheila rushed over, "I'm SO sorry," she said to the people, "Misty's ruined your game now."

"Never mind," a lady replied, "it's been a first that's for sure!" More laughter.

Sheila came striding up to me. I thought I would run off – she'd never catch me on this great ship with all the hidey-holes I would find, but there again, I looked at her face – perhaps I'd better not! I'd had my bit of fun. So, obediently, I walked up to the lady who had been playing the game and dropped the little ball at her feet. She clapped her hands and gave me a pat.

"Well," she said in a drawling accent, "how cute is that – isn't she just so adorable?" So ... I didn't really get into trouble but Sheila marched me straight back to the stateroom, gave me my lunch and went off on her own. I retired outside to the balcony and spent the rest of the day out there dozing.

Sheila came and went a few times during the day, changing into another outfit and muttering something about having to look elegant for afternoon tea, and then later in the evening she took me to the theatre again and we watched a spectacular singing and dancing show which I really enjoyed. I like your human mewsic on the whole though it's not as good, of course, as our local cats' chorus club which meets on the back wall of next door's garden once a month. After the show it was a quick visit to the casino, where Sheila was all smiles because she came away with a profit, and the final drink of the day ... yes you've guessed it! Amoretto latte!

DAY 6

Today we arrived at another island and from the balcony it looked really beautiful in the sun but, if anything, it was even hotter. "Well, Misty," said Sheila, "here we are at my favourite island, Madeira." Oh, I suppose that's why you like it, dear, for its cakes.

After we got off the ship, we got onto a bus (can't say I've ever been on one of them before, but it was much bigger than Tony's taxi.) and then we arrived at a hill where there were strange looking objects like small, round, glass rooms hanging on wires – with people sitting inside them – being moved up the side of the hill. I wasn't sure I liked the look of them. Oh dear, were we going to get inside one of them too? I shivered despite the heat. It seemed we were but Sheila picked me up and carried me on with her sitting me on her lap so I felt safer. Off we started and feeling more confident I looked out and marvelled at the view from being so high up. I'd never been so high in my life before. Now I knew how birds must feel. This certainly beat sitting in a tree – what a great experience. I was becoming totally addicted now to cruising and seeing sights I would never see back home – no wonder Sheila loves it so. Arriving at the top there was a definite drop in temperature but it was still hotter than it ever gets in Cornwall. I wondered what was going to happen next and how we would get back down to the ground again. I was soon to find out. Sheila followed a crowd of other people and, after passing some more shops and walking down a winding road for a while, we came to a place where there were some strange looking vehicles that looked like wicker baskets on skis. What on earth? Waiting our turn, we got into one, Sheila sitting me on her lap again and very firmly gripping both my collar and my lead. Two young men then came up behind us and started pushing us along the road. What a weird thing to happen, I was a bit purrplexed.

"Hang on to your hat, Misty!" said Sheila gripping me even tighter. What was she on about, hat? I don't wear a hat! Suddenly, the road seemed to slip away downwards, the guys behind jumped up onto the back of the basket and we suddenly rocketed down the road. OMG, was I terrified? Mind you, even Sheila was screeching as we whizzed round the bends as the road sloped ever more steeply downwards. My fur was literally standing on end. But a few minutes later thankfully we arrived at the end of this purrfect nightmare and Sheila stepped off, setting me down on to firm ground again. Phew, we were both feeling a bit wobbly after that! NOT an experience I wish to repeat.

After that Sheila needed another frothy coffee and I just needed a sit down. There was a café nearby so we retired there before going back to the ship again. What a day! Still, another experience I could notch up to brag about to the other cats at home. I wouldn't admit to them, of course, how I had been shaken rigid by the wicker basket fiasco.

Back at the comparative calm of the stateroom, we both looked in surprise at a big vase of flowers that had appeared on the table. Beside it was a card which Sheila read that put a smile on her face.

"That's nice," she said, "tomorrow night I am to dine at the Captain's table. Top Cat to you Misty! Though he won't be there himself, it'll be hosted by a guy I haven't met before, the fleet food and beverage director." Oooh, get you, I thought. Well now she'll be spending half the day tomorrow deciding what to wear I suppose. So much easier for a cat – just wearing one outfit for all occasions! I went out to the litter box and then back for my lunchtime snack and she went off to have hers I suppose. Apart from another stroll on the grass above followed by a sit down on the opposite side from where the people were playing their ball games (I wonder why she chose that side for us to sit!) we did nothing else that afternoon. When Sheila went to get her pre-dinner drinks at the Passport Bar she took me with her. Whilst she perched on a high chair by the bar, I sat underneath as usual. Looking up I could hear her talking to another passenger who had just arrived at the bar. She seemed to be admiring his shirt. Well, he did look very smart! Although he was speaking in purrfect English he, too, had a strange accent I'd never heard before. Wonder where he comes from? I thought. Sheila must have been telling him about me because he leant down and gave me a pat on the head.

"Hi Misty," he said, "I'm pleased to meet you. I like cats too and I have one at home called Micha." Nice, I thought and turned on the purr switch.

"This is Juan," said Sheila and he comes from Peru." Purroo eh? No wonder he likes cats, there must be lots of them living in a place called THAT! They sat there chatting and drinking for the next hour and then he went off to have his dinner and she took me back to the stateroom and went to get hers. Tonight she had ordered lobster chunks in a tasty sauce for me – yummy!

I didn't see Sheila until much later as she didn't take me to the show saying it was a comedian, not music, so I wouldn't be interested. Well, I told you earlier about when I saw a comedian on the last trip. He'd stood all alone on the stage talking about, I don't know what, but all the people watching were laughing at him. How humiliating for him. I had felt so sorry for him – how awful he must have felt. So, NO, I didn't want to see another comedian, thank you. When Shelia did eventually return I thought we were going to bed but she clipped on the lead and said we were off to the casino to see if her luck was in I doubted it. But I was wrong. We met up with her friends, Val and Ken, and all three of them sat at the noisy machines and in the end Sheila and Val's were noisier than Ken's so it seemed that the ladies had won and he hadn't. Better luck next time mate! So he went off to bed and Sheila and Val, with me dragging along behind, had a celebratory drink at another of the many bars on this ship. This one seemed to have its top made of ice – yes real freezing ice – and the guys behind it were making strange (to me anyway) cocks' tails called Martinis. They were also throwing bottles into the air and catching them and the passengers were clapping and oohing and aahing at their antics. All very clever if you like that kind of thing, I suppose, but too noisy for me. I spent the entire time underneath Sheila's chair. Still, we weren't there too long and then it was back home again, to bed.

DAY 7

This turned out to be quite a boring day for me but a good one for Sheila, as far as I could make out. We had arrived at the first of the Canary Islands and I was really looking forward to seeing clouds of yellow birds flying overhead. First thing in the morning I went and looked over the balcony edge but, although the usual big white sea birds were hanging about, not a canary was to be seen. Never mind, I thought, maybe we'll see them when we get off. After breakfast, and when Del had done all his work, Sheila returned and said that she wasn't taking me off the ship today because she was going to a big department store in the town to do some shopping and so she couldn't take me with her. Well, I wasn't upset about missing a shopping trip but what about my bird watching plans? So I felt a sulk coming on and stomped over to my bed and sat in it staring at the wall.

"Now don't get the hump, Misty" she said, "I'll bring you something nice from the pet department. Go and sit on the balcony." And then she was off. Thanks a lot, dear. I went into the non-bathroom and vent my feelings out on a towel and then out I went and spent the rest of the morning lying in the sunshine. Each day seemed to be getting hotter than the one before. But it was nice. Soon sleep overtook me.

Lunchtime came and went … no Sheila. But Del appeared with a plate of food for me and, unfortunately, he went into the

70

non-bathroom and he DID spot the ruined towel, which I had in my temper forgotten to disguise. Whoops! But he laughed and just said they had plenty more towels and he would bring another one, and if I promised not to do it again he wouldn't tell Sheila. Well, I knew he was a good sort of guy. But I wasn't going to promise anything.

It was nearly time for the afternoon trip to the coffee lounge before madam returned, carrying several large bags but not, I was relieved to see, a teddy bear. Oh, I forgot to tell you, she did get a small one in Madeira at one of the shops near the wicker basket run.

"Here's a new collar for tonight, Misty, as it's formal night," she said, "how do you like it?" Haven't I got enough collars? I'd rather have had some tasty treats. But I had to admit it was certainly very – dark pink velvet studded with sparkly stones. I didn't put on my happy face and so she then laughed and said, "Go on then, Misty, I know these are what you really wanted." And she produced a box of delicious tiny cheese balls which she brings me home every time she goes on her travels as they don't seem to make them in England. After eating a couple I cheered up and off we went to the coffee lounge.

As I said earlier, it was a rather boring day for me. Afternoon coffee session over, we went back to the stateroom and I retreated to the balcony and its sunshine again whilst Sheila fussed around doing this and that inside, though she joined me for a while before she said that, as it was formal night, she would order me something really special for my dinner. Well, I was up for that! It turned out to be bits of something called caviar followed by a kind of fish stew. I think it had a posh

71

name but I forget it. Whatever, it was pretty good but it took quite a lot of whisker washing afterwards. When Del came in later he also gave me one of those giant shrimps so, all in all, the day might have been boring but the food wasn't! Sheila got herself all dolled up and went off to her posh dinner party, first meeting up with her fellow guests in another of the bars on the ship. Then I think she must have gone to a show because it seemed quite late when she returned, clutching a red rose and a large picture of her and everyone at the table. She has loads of pictures like it on her study walls at home. Does she really need another one?

"Come on, Misty," she smiled, "let's finish off a very good evening by seeing if my luck is still in at the casino." Oh, must we? She put on my new collar, and it had a matching lead, and off we went. I must say looking around everybody seemed to be dressed up, looking a lot better than when I'd seen them on the outside deck or round the pool.

We got to the casino and it was very crowded but we didn't see Val or Ken or anybody else there that Sheila knew and also somebody was sitting at her favourite machine that she had won on before. Whoops! She found another one and sat down. I crept under the seat trying to get away from all the noise. Well, for about ten minutes jangle, jangle, whirr, whirr went the machine when she pressed its buttons, and I thought well dear, you're not going to get lucky with this machine! But suddenly its music got louder and a voice that seemed to come from inside it said something that sounded like, "fifteen free spins." I came out from my hidey hole and saw that the machine was going mad spinning its little picture reels round and round all by itself. Sheila was just sitting back watching open mouthed. I watched too. And her luck had stayed with her. She won nearly $400! So that finished off a very good day for her.

"Goodness Misty," she said, "I can't believe it!

I am not going to let the machine take it back off me, so let's go!" And we did – back to the lovely quiet stateroom and bed!

DAY 8

At last I got to go ashore in the next Canary Island called Gran Canaria. Oh, that sounded good, like the little canary birds were perhaps big canary birds on this island? We got off the ship and I eagerly looked all around me but not a yellow canary was to be seen … anywhere! We walked along a pathway where I could see blue sparkling water on one side and on the other, trees and all sorts of buildings. I told you that each day had seemed hotter than the one before, but here it was not just hot but also very, very sort of sticky air (I heard Sheila saying to some other people who were also walking alongside us that it was humid, a word from your language that I'm afraid I've not come across before!) and they all agreed. Very, very humid. All of their faces were dripping and my fur felt all claggy. After plodding along until we were nearly at the town, we came to some seats and they decided to take a breather. I flopped out feeling as exhausted as they all seemed to be. I like hot, but I've discovered I don't like humid. Whilst we were sitting there and they were mopping their brows, one of the guys asked about me and so Sheila told them how I was a cat author(!) and got the usual replies. Pats all round followed, which felt nice on my now very sticky fur coat.

"Yes," continued Sheila, "and Misty thinks there are lots of canaries living on the islands so she's hoping to spot a few!"

Lots of laughs followed.

"Doesn't she know that the Canary Islands were, in fact, named after dogs?" said the man. What! Dogs, never! Surely not!

"Oh dear," said Sheila, "I've never spoilt her illusions and told her that. Now you've well and truly let the cat out of the bag." More laughter followed. I was gobsmacked as you humans say. I couldn't believe that stupid dogs had islands named after them. I glared up at Sheila. "OK, OK, Misty," she said, "it's not the end of the world. Come on, let's press on into town, I could do with a cold drink."

The others agreed so Sheila yanked on the lead and off we went again, with me not in the best of tempers what with the humid air and now having learnt that, for once, cats had lost out to dogs big time. Let alone that I wouldn't see any delicious little yellow canaries flying around.

Eventually, we arrived at the main town and, to her dismay, Sheila found that all the shops were shut, including the big store she liked, because it was a Sunday. She knew that, of course, but had expected at least a few to be open, but all that there was were a few outside stands along by the beachside. So she wasn't in the best of humours either as we made our way up the main street until we found a coffee place, where we sat down at an outside table in the shade. For once, Sheila didn't have a hot frothy coffee but a cold iced coffee. The nice lady there gave me a bowl of water too. We sat in silence each brooding over our disappointments of the day – no shopping for her and no canaries for me!

Back to the ship again and its blessed air conditioning. Lunch and then to the coffee lounge where Sheila chatted to Randy who had some time on his hands because so many people were ashore (they obviously didn't mind humid!). Then it was much as usual ... after my quite early dinner, Sheila took me with her to the Passport Bar and we met up with the nice guy from Purroo again, then she brought me back and went off for her own dinner. When Del came in to do his evening duties he looked at the towels hanging up and all seemed neat and tidy (as I'd made sure they would be!) so with a "Good girl" to me, he went off satisfied. Sheila returned and we went off to the theatre where there was another music show that I enjoyed – a man playing a piano and singing jolly songs. Then she said we were going to the coffee lounge again to meet with Juan from Purroo as he, too, liked Amoretto and she had told him that Hanns would make him a delicious cup of coffee mixed with the sickly stuff. It turned out that Hanns lived somewhere near Purroo and he, like Juan, was very particular and only ever wanted to drink the absolute best coffee because their countries were where coffee actually grew. So they were both experts! Juan then explained to Hanns exactly how he wanted his made talking in a totally different language. It sounded like a lot of gibberish to me.

"Go on," laughed Sheila, "you can say what you want about me, I won't understand a word of it." They laughed and then talked in English again for the rest of the time we were there.

Two or three cups of coffee and Amoretto later, Sheila said her goodbyes and arranged to meet up with Juan in a day or two's time at the senior officers' cocks tail party, if they'd not met at the bar before then. We set off to the elevators but, just as we got there, Darren and the guy called Guy who had lots of guest relations stepped out. More cat banter between the two of them and Sheila. Guy picked me up and gave me a cuddle, telling me he missed his own two cats, and how he was pleased to meet me at last. What a nice guy Guy is I thought rubbing my face across his cheek. As he must know what cats like best, maybe next time we meet he might bring me a nice treat … one can only hope! I did hear Darren suggesting the three of them meet up when they had some spare time later on. They wandered off and we got in the elevator, and when we arrived at the stateroom and Sheila opened the door she simply burst into her best laughing hyena impression.

I told you she had bought a teddy bear from Madeira and she has another little one from home that travels everywhere with her. I've heard her tell friends back home that he has travelled many, many thousands of miles all over the world. Oh well, it'll take a month of Sundays for me to catch HIM up I guess! Still I'm on my way – two cruises now equal a few thousand miles at least. Each evening Del placed Sheila's favourite chocolates on the bed pillows and tonight he had also moved the two teddy bears so one was sitting on the bed, and one was sitting on the pillow. Each had a chocolate in its paw and the one on the pillow was also holding the TV remote control and playing on the TV was the cartoon channel which both bears were watching most intently (thought I didn't hear them laughing!). Sheila just creased up and it even made me smile. She was still giggling when we finally went to bed.

DAY 9

It started off with one of those things I think you call a coincidence! At about 5.15 a.m. in the morning, both Sheila and I were woken up by the sound of the TV. She jumped out of bed thinking it was some sort of emergency and perhaps each stateroom was being contacted. But no, just a normal channel was playing. It's those naughty bears was my first thought. Even Sheila looked at them but the remote control was sitting quietly by itself nowhere near the bears and, in fact, not even facing towards the TV anyway. Most puzzling! She went through the channels on the TV but there was nothing alarming, it was just on. So she switched it off and we both went back to sleep again. Later in the morning when she'd come back from having her breakfast she said she had mentioned to some other people about this and it had happened to their TVs as well (so it wasn't those bears!). It seemed that there had been something she called 'an electrical spike' which had caused all the TVs to start up automatically from standby. I wasn't quite sure what she was talking about, but then I am not a technocat!

Today, we were at another Canary Island that had no canaries, called Fuerteventura and here it was even more humid and hot than yesterday. Sheila and I felt we were walking through a desert on the way to the town there. We sat outside a café with me under the table trying to keep in the shade and she was alternately wiping her face and taking sips from a tall glass full of ice and some sickly looking orange coloured drink. Suddenly, along the street came a group of young people looking as if they'd come from a circus. One was walking on big sticks that made him about 10 feet tall, one was throwing bottle shaped things in the air – five at a time, and catching them again – and the third was blowing big bubbles which children nearby were trying to catch. I would have liked to have tried to catch some too, but in the humid heat, just couldn't be bothered. My fur seemed to feel twice as heavy as normal and sort of damp so all I wanted to do was loll about. Lots of people were watching the circus performers who gradually walked on up the street towards the town centre.

"Well, we'll just go on up the street a bit ourselves," said Sheila, "but I'm not going far in this heat. Just to see if there's a souvenir shop somewhere so maybe I will be able to find a bear from here." Not a good reason to move, I thought, but had no option as she tugged on the lead. So we went, at a very slow pace, a bit further along the street to where there was a big souvenir shop. No bears though, so she ended up with a little camel that had 'Fuerteventura' on its side. It seemed this island was home to lots of camels (well it had struck us that it seemed like a desert!) and that's why there were no souvenir teddies, but souvenir camels instead. We trudged on to where the street ended in a large circular area with other streets leading off it, but that was as far as we went, thank goodness! Too hot, too humid! I think Sheila was having withdrawal symptoms because she'd not done much shopping, but at least her wallet was happy. She did go in one shop more on the way back – a huge place full of those bottles of sweet sickly smelling stuff you like to sprinkle on yourselves. Yuk! She bought a bottle for herself and also one for Randy because Hanns had told her last night it was his birthday. Then it was a slow walk back to the lovely cool ship and a quick wipe down for Sheila's face(!) and a lie down for me.

After lunch we were in the coffee place again and Sheila gave Randy his bottle of smelly stuff which he was delighted with and, another coincidence, the brand was his favourite. She'd had no idea, but knew it was one that most male humans liked. So smiles all round! After that it was just as normal really … I slept for the rest of the afternoon before I had my delicious (lamb cutlet) dinner and went with Sheila to the bar for her own pre dinner drink, and then after she'd been to dinner she took me along to the theatre to see a really great show. It was her favourite kind of music – think she calls it rock or pop or something – and all the other people watching were cheering and singing along with the group that was playing. They seemed to be taking off some world famous group that had a name that sounded very royal. Can you guess who they were? Even I felt like getting up and dancing about too, though sitting on Sheila's knee which was moving up and down to the beat of the music, I didn't need to!

Afterwards we went along to the casino. Surely, she's not going to be lucky again, I thought. Val and Ken were there again and this time he was looking a bit happier because he had won and Val wasn't because she hadn't. Sheila sat down next to them and they chattered on about this and that … boring, boring! If the casino hadn't been so noisy I would have soon nodded off. But this time Sheila wasn't lucky and her steak ran out in about 10 minutes so she told the others she was going to drown her sorrows in Amoretto and we left. On the way we bumped into Tim from the gym. He was also going to the coffee place so we went with him. I settled myself down under their table and they were talking.

Suddenly, I heard Sheila say, "I don't believe it!" It turned out that he lived in Cornwall like us. Another of your coincidences – well you say things come in three's don't you? And when Hanns brought their frothy drinks I saw his was also the dreaded Amoretto mix. Just what is it about this stuff? Even the smell of it made me want to throw up. Tim was asking Sheila if she was going to go to the 'dancing with the officers' event the next night but she said, "no way"; she had two left feet.

"Go on," he said, "it's always a laugh, some people are very good but there's always plenty of rubbish ones for everyone to laugh at."

"Well, I'd certainly be one of those," said Sheila. Yes, you would dear. Miaow! Miaow! "Right, we're off."

"See you again," said Tim patting me, "Do try and persuade Misty to come to the gym again, there might be something else she'd like to try … ha ha!" You'll be lucky mate!

DAY 10

The last of the Canary Islands; Lanzarote. It was still very humid but not quite so bad as yesterday. Very, very hot though. We walked, slowly, around a lake and stopped on the bridge that crossed it looking at small fish darting about in the water below. It was so hot that I wondered if the fish weren't cooking and that some enterprising person wasn't hooking them out of the water straight onto plates, adding some of those chips you like to eat, and making himself a fortune. Arriving in the town, needless to say Sheila's first stop was for a coffee and then I was dragged along with her in and out of the shops. No bears here either so another camel came to join the one from Fuerteventura. As we arrived back at the ship we saw Sheila's friend, Mary, and she said that she and Eric had been for a ride on a camel on their tour around the island. "Well we just did a tour round the shops," said Sheila.

"Why doesn't that surprise me?" replied Mary. They all laughed.

After lunch we went up onto the grass deck again and this time nobody was playing with balls but petite Sam and Maarten seemed to be teaching people how to wave their arms and legs about and bend their bodies into odd positions. All this seemed to be in slow motion. Sheila linked my lead around a chair leg and I lay down and watched as she joined in. Seemed pretty pointless to me, but at the end of the session I heard Sheila saying to Sam how she'd enjoyed it … she'd never tried yoga before and now felt very calm and serene. Perhaps I should try it, I mewsed, or there again, perhaps not. I didn't think I would be able to cross my four legs like they did. I think I would end up in a horrible tangle. Strolling around, we went past the one place on the ship that I really did not like. I think it was called the hot glass show or something. Last time Sheila took me to watch, it frightened me because there were flames coming out of a box at the back and two people, holding what looked like long tubes with blobs of coloured stuff on the ends, seemed to be blowing down them and twisting them at the same time. Everyone watching was oohing and aahing as every few moments the shapeless coloured blobs turned into bowls or vases. Weird and clever but I didn't like the hissing noises or the flame. This time, Sheila didn't stop. She must have remembered how I felt about the place. After stopping for an ice cream to cool us down, we went back to the stateroom.

Then it was the same routine for me but she went off early for her dinner as she said Peng Fei was taking her to eat at the 'quirky' restaurant (yes, quirky, that's a good word isn't it?). I added it to my vocabulary last time as she had used it to describe the special eating place he had taken her to. She said she had never been to a place like it and loved it, so he was taking her on this trip too. Well, he's such a kind guy…

So I spent the evening sleeping. Well, we cats do like to try to sleep for 20 hours out of 24 if we can, and I had a few hours to catch up on. Sheila arrived back, switched on the TV and looked at the news, carried out her duties in the litter tray department, then did her own ablutions and that was that.

Another sea day tomorrow she told me and then we would arrive at a lovely city called Lisbon. Bring it on!

DAY 11

Another day dawned hot and sunny but thankfully not humid. Sparkling blue waters all round us and matching sky above. I stretched flat out on the balcony and thought I wish this cruise could go on forever! Del was making that whistling sound like the birds make as he did his morning duties, and he stopped beside me for a few moments also admiring the view.

"I theenk you're liking this, Mistee," he smiled and tickled my tummy. Oh yes, I sure am! He threw a handful of my fishy treats onto the decking and went off. Lovely, I'll eat those in a moment, I thought.

Suddenly, I jumped as a shadow blotted out the sun and a huge black sea bird zoomed in and landed right by me. It certainly wasn't the usual white ones I'd seen before, and they were large enough. This one was just scarily massive. It had an evil looking sharp beak and its red eyes glared at me. It had big feet too, with nasty looking talons on its toes. For a fleeting moment I thought this is what a mouse must feel like when it's cornered by a cat. I gulped and cringed back against the wall. Del, Sheila – where are you when I need you? The bird looked at me but then noticed the pile of treats and, fortunately, must have thought they were more tempting than a piece of cat, so scoffed the lot in about two seconds and then with a backward sneering glance over its shoulder took off and flew away. I rushed straight back into the stateroom just as Sheila entered from the other end. I collapsed on my bed, my teeth chattering and my heart beating like the sound of raindrops battering against a window in a storm.

"Whatever's the matter, Misty" Sheila asked, "you're shaking like a leaf." She knelt down and stroked me and then picked me up and sat me on her knee giving me a comforting hug. She looked all around. "What's scared you?" she said, looking out on the balcony. "There's nothing out there." Oh, but there WAS, there was!

"Well, whatever it was, everything's OK now" Sheila said, "come on I'll take you with me to the trivia session, you'll soon cheer up!" She clipped on the lead, and for once I felt glad to be secured to her, NO giant bird would get me with her there. We went up to the big room above where all the groups were sitting waiting for the questions to start and I felt much safer here. We sat down with the rest of the Sea Legs team and I sat watching but determined not to nod off in case I had a nightmare about the big black bird. It seemed that Sea Legs had their own nightmare because they got stumped by several of the questions today and ended up twelfth in the list. So, at the end of the session, while I had cheered up, they certainly hadn't!

We went outside for an ice cream afterwards and, although I looked nervously about me, there was no sign of the bird thank goodness. We sat down and Sheila was talking to the people beside her and I heard them ask her if she had seen the group of frigate birds fly past earlier? She said she hadn't but looked down at me and said, "Ah, but I think Misty may have – she was terrified by something this morning, it could have been them." Frigate birds eh? I'll remember that name, that's for sure!

After lunch we went outside again to the pool deck. I can see no fun whatsoever in getting wet and I've spent my life making sure I don't(!) but you lot obviously love it because, whenever we've walked around the decks, the water pools are always full of people. This time there were crowds of people standing round a pool watching some of the ship's officers having some sort of ball game. It seemed there was a competition and the winning team would then play against a team of passengers.

Sheila joined the crowd and she let me perch myself on the back of a nearby chair so I could see the fun too! Well, I don't mind seeing anyone else getting wet as long as I don't have to. Tim and Maarten were in charge of the match and were strutting around looking important and blowing whistles from time to time. Maarten wasn't thrilling the ladies by wearing his tight drainpipe trousers, both he and Tim were in matching navy blue outfits of vests and shorts, the officers were in white. I couldn't see the two officers I had met, Darren and Guy, in the team but maybe they didn't like getting themselves wet either. There was lots of cheering from the crowd if one of the teams scored a point with the volleyball they were hurling about. After a breather and a cold drink the winning team then played against some of the passengers. The cheering and shouting got even more heated during this final match but in the end, somehow, the passengers won. The officers trailed off looking dejected and the crowd surrounded their victorious friends laughing and patting them on the back and some of them even got pushed back into the pool again. I retreated swiftly and jumped back on the ground, I didn't want to get soaked. I'd had a nasty experience of getting wet on the last trip when I was innocently sitting on the balcony and got half drowned when suddenly a machine had whirred by overhead sending shoots of water to clean the glass doors. Not a pleasant memory! It was all Sheila's fault. The night before she had been left a card saying that window cleaning was to take place but she forgot about it and so left the doors open a crack so I could get through as normal. I will say no more on the subject...

Going back in the elevator, we saw Juan and he reminded Sheila that they were going to the officers' cocks tail party that evening so they arranged a time to meet. "Sorry, I can't take you to that, Misty," said Sheila when we got back to the stateroom, "there'll be too many people there and, anyway, I know you only drink milk and water, and there'll certainly be none of that there! Well, I certainly hope not!" she added.

Dinner for me was chicken liver pate followed by fillet of sole cut into chunks. Very tasty. I gave the towel its daily attack (I was now hiding my tracks very successfully!) then jumped up on my cushion on the sofa and had a nice whisker licking session and an all over stretch. Cat yoga maybe? I never knew what Sheila had to eat for her dinner because, of course, I wasn't allowed in the dining room by those spoilsports in elf and safety, but I think it was probably a lot better than she has at home – stuff she just puts into a magic cabinet in the kitchen for about five minutes.

When she came back she fussed around getting ready for the drinks party and with a quick pat for me promised she'd be back later to take me to the show because there was a guy on she'd seen before who she thought I would like. A while later she came back and said the party had been great and she'd met up with Juan there and she had chatted with Darren and Guy who were still bantering on about purple cats and stuff. She said they were going to meet up with us the day after tomorrow so that would be nice, I liked them – cat people! She put another of my evening collars on me, and off we went to the theatre to meet Juan and go to the show. On the way she stopped at one of the shops selling those sparkly ornament things you love to wear and it seemed she knew the guy who was in charge there too. But whenever she'd been in the shop before I hadn't been with her. His name was Gabriel and, believe it or not, (here's another coincidence!) he also lived in Purroo. But he didn't have a cat. Shame! He did say how pretty I was and what a lovely collar I had on. I purred up at him, yes of course I had a lovely collar – I have lots of them – Sheila was as fussy about how I looked in the evenings as she was with her own appearance.

"How about buying Misty a diamond bracelet I have here," said Gabriel, "it would be just right for her and fit round her neck perfectly," he laughed. Yes, that would be nice I thought, and pawed expectantly at his leg.

"You have to be joking," giggled Sheila, "a cat wearing a $1,000 collar!"

"Well, I was," chuckled Gabriel, "but you'd be surprised how many famous people would put a diamond collar on their cat!"

"Yeah, well I'm not that famous," responded Sheila and they both turned on their hyena laughing switches. We walked on to the theatre with me feeling a bit put out that I wouldn't get a diamond collar. Still, I guess my pink one with its fake sparkly stones would have to do. I sighed.

But then we met up with Juan at the theatre and he patted me and gave me a nice ear tickle so I brightened up again. I sat between him and Sheila and looked expectantly at the stage below. What were we going to see? On to the stage came a guy and he was throwing all sorts of things into the air and catching them, and at the same time making the people watching scream with laughter at the things he was saying, but as I didn't understand what he was saying it didn't impress me much and I didn't think Juan seemed too impressed either. But then the man did something that needed no words. He produced one of those machines with two big wheels like I had seen in the gym that you like to sit on (and get yourselves nowhere fast!) but his machine only had one wheel and its seat was fixed on to a very long pole on top. He got three men from the audience to join him and the last ten minutes of his show was spent with them trying to ride this strange thing, prop it up or even get on it – none of which they could do! But it really was funny to see. Sheila and Juan and the people around us were all imitating those hyenas and, I must say, if I could laugh, well I would have! If I had been on the stage myself, I could have run straight up the pole in a couple of seconds and sat on the seat. I would have been the star of the show. Still smiling, the audience left the theatre and Sheila, Juan and I made our way to the coffee lounge where they downed their coffee and Amorettos and I had an ankle watch. The next day was the visit to the place called Lisbon and it seemed Juan was going on a tour to some very old town nearby whilst Sheila was going on a tour of some new shops. Nothing for me to look forward to then. Goodnights said, it was back to the stateroom and bed.

DAY 12

Sheila woke me up earlier than usual and said we had to go out on the balcony pretty quickly as we were just about to go under Lisbon's famous bridge. She picked me up and because we were on a high deck, as we went under the bridge, looking up, I thought the ship would never get under the bottom of it. It looked as if the gap between the top of the ship and the bridge was only a couple of feet. But we made it and as we carried on slowly up the river towards the dock, Sheila looked back and suddenly dropped me and quickly ran in to get her little picture making machine. Just as she pointed it at the bridge, I saw on a level underneath the road where the motor machines were crossing, a long, snake-like machine with about ten compartments that seemed to be running on rails, and then suddenly overhead in the sky appeared one of those flying winged machines. Sheila punched the air and said "Well, that was just SO lucky! Cars, a train and a plane all at the same time! Yeah!" I wasn't sure why she thought it was lucky, I thought it was black cats that were lucky!

After our respective morning ablutions and breakfasts off we went into Lisbon. We got one of those big buses, like we'd been on in Madeira, from the side of the ship into the centre of the town. I think Sheila called it what sounded like a sittee, not a town, but I may have been wrong. Well, it was pretty big and there were so many people about, it was a bit intimidating for little me, so I stayed close to Sheila's side. Again, I saw lots of little dogs being carried around in ladies' bags. I wondered why they didn't walk like the dogs do in Cornwall. Maybe our dogs at home are poor so have to walk everywhere and these here were rich and lazy ... they probably wore diamond collars too! The only big dog we saw was a St Bernard and Sheila stopped to stroke it and talk to its owner as she used to have a St Bernard called Hennessy. He was before my time but I remember my predecessor, Truffles, telling me how gentle and loveable he was and how she sometimes used to sleep curled up on his back at night time. Aaah! I must say this St Bernard looked lovely too and we even touched noses.

Soon we arrived at an outside café and Sheila sat down and said to the guy, who came up with a cup of – yes, you've guessed it – frothy coffee, that she came to this café every year and especially liked their custard tarts, a Portuguese favourite. He brought her two, and eating them she made a right mess dropping crumbs everywhere. Irritated in case they dropped onto my fur I sat up but the crumbs had brought three or four pigeons right over to us. Phew, I nearly had a convulsion – was I going to be within reaching distance of a bird at last? I lunged forward and brushed the wing of the nearest pigeon, who barely glanced up from pecking away at the crumbs. What? Didn't I scare him in the least? I lunged out with my other paw and this time he returned my lunge with a swipe from his beak. Cheeky bird, I'll give him what for I thought. I pulled forward again but this time Sheila hauled me back so hard I thought I was going to be strangled. "Stay back, Misty," she snapped, "don't you dare..." Then one of the other pigeons came up behind me and pecked at my tail and another two charged at me from the side (the first one was still sweeping up the crumbs!) and so I swiped wildly at them all with claws at full stretch. I did manage to catch one or two of their tail feathers but not the birds themselves, this lot were pretty vicious and didn't seem at all scared. Ridiculous! All birds are supposed to be frightened of cats! I growled and hissed but that didn't seem to have any effect either. Then one of them pecked my paw. Ow! I totally lost it then – my temper was up now and I turned from a sweet demure little cat into a hissing, growling ball of fury. I struggled to pull away from Sheila and give this bird gang something they'd remember. They were all swearing at me now and I was swearing at them, but the trouble with being small is that you can be picked up easily by someone big, and Sheila did just that and gave me a really sharp tap on the nose. I was furious now; she had humiliated me in front of these birds. I hissed at her but got another tap on the nose. She shooed the birds away – they took notice of her – and still holding me she apologised to the waiter for disturbing the peace, paid her bill and stamped off up the street dragging me along behind her. Both of us had scowls on our faces now and the happy mood of before had totally gone, AND my paw was hurting. We came to a seat and Sheila sat down with me cowering behind her feet. I was expecting a real telling off because we don't have moments like this between us, really we don't. It was quite out of character for both of us. But after a few moments, nothing happened and I dared to look up at her.

"Oh, Misty," she said picking me up, "I'm sorry I told you off so, but I thought you were going to hurt those birds." (Huh! It was ME they hurt!) "Let's calm down now," she continued, "and we'll forget it ever happened." OK then, I agreed. We sat in the sun for a few minutes more and then, both feeling happier now, started walking again.

On up the street we went and arrived at a large shop selling handbags. Oh no – bags, as well as teddy bears, are an irresistible force to Sheila, so true to form she added another to her collection. A little further on I blinked, was that a cow I could see standing outside a shop? One of those lovely creatures that provides my daily milk, but surely they live in green grassy fields, not in a busy street. As we got closer, yes it was definitely a black and white cow. But when we got right up to it, no it was just a model of a cow. But it looked very real. "This'll make a funny photo," smiled Sheila, and put me on the cow's back taking out her little picture making machine. Whilst I was perched on the cow's back several other passersby took pics as well. Well, I love having my picture taken so my good humour was now fully restored.

Sheila only went into one more shop, thank goodness, and came out with a bag full of another of her favourite things; chocolate covered marzipan sweets. Sickly and disgusting, yuk – something that would make me throw up if I had one, but she's never let me near her chocolate anyway as it is apparently a very bad thing for cats. Good for humans, deadly for cats. So we returned to the ship, had our respective lunches and it was back to the usual afternoon routine again. I was well and truly getting into the shipboard way of life but there were now only two more days to go and then it would be back home again. Still, I would have so many things to remember and, of course,

I would be sharing my thoughts with you by writing this book.

The ship left the dockside just as I was eating my dinner and Sheila said she would do a bit of packing as she never liked leaving it to the last day which she liked to keep totally free to say her goodbyes to her friends. Purrsonally, I don't know why she didn't just stick her clothes into her case at the end of each day – after all, she never seemed to wear the same outfit twice! But then you humans never have the logic of cats. We went outside and watched as we sailed under the big bridge, but there were only motor machines crossing it this time. I saw a big model of a human with outstretched arms standing on the river bank and Sheila took a picture of him too. I'd noticed that all over Lisbon there were lots of models, mainly of men riding horses, but none as big as the man by the bridge.

As purr usual now, we met up with Juan at the Passport Bar before he went off for his dinner and Sheila to hers and then we all met up again and went to the theatre. This time there was a young lady singer on. It seemed from the way Sheila and Juan were talking that he knew a lot about music and played it himself on a piano machine. He laughed when Sheila told him that at school she had tried to learn another instrument called a violin but it had been a total disaster. To her parents it sounded as if she was stamping on a cat (not an expression I'd heard before and I hope nobody would ever stamp on me, but if they did so, my screeching would be unbelievable!) so after a few weeks they had taken the violin away from her. Sadly, neither Sheila nor Juan seemed to appreciate the singer's efforts and, I must say, neither did I. After the show, we went to the coffee lounge and they talked and talked and it was so boring I just fell asleep. However, I woke up as they bid each other, and Hanns, good night and once back in the stateroom I went straight to bed and continued the pleasant dream I'd been having where I was hurling lots of pigeons about.

DAY 13

Morning spent just as usual for me really, though Sheila did take me with her to the progressive trivia thing and they ended by climbing up the leader board to seventh so that put smiles on Sea Legs' faces. It was the final session tomorrow so they would be all out to get to the top. No chance, I thought. Miaow! Miaow! Then we met up with the cat loving officers Darren and Guy. Darren, giving a hyena laugh, gave Sheila a present of a pack of cards with pictures of cats on them and said they were going to all play a game with them. Sheila had never seen this game before and certainly not a pack with pictures of cats on it. They sat round a table by some place called a bustro, or was it bistro? And it seemed they had to try to trump each other's cat cards. Whatever that meant! They were still bantering about cats and I saw some of the other passengers looking at us and probably thinking they were all mad. What made Sheila really laugh was when Guy said he knew someone who called their cat a name that sounded like Cat-mandu. Odd! Then she made them both go aaah by telling them a true story she had been told by an Amerrycan man passenger.

It seemed this man and his family had five large golden Retriever or Labrador dogs (she wasn't sure exactly which as the man referred to them just as Goldens) but no cat. In their back door was a dog door so the dogs could go in and out to the back yard whenever they wished. One day there was a lot of noise at the dog door and the man saw the five dogs were all barking and staring as a little black cat walked in through the dog door. The man and the dogs remained transfixed as the cat did a tour of the ground floor of the house, looking into each room, and then calmly walked back outside again. Some hours later the man heard the dogs barking again and went to the door to see the cat coming back in again and this time it was dragging a little blanket behind it. The cat moved itself in with them (well, they do say cats choose their owners don't they?) and it turned out it was a lady cat. She lived with them for about five years and one afternoon she just picked up her blanket and walked out and they never saw her again. Well, I thought, she probably had had enough of living with five big slobbery dogs and had found another place to live. Lovely story though!

Later we returned to the stateroom and Sheila found a message that we should meet with China boy, Peng Fei, tomorrow afternoon (the last day, boo hoo!). She did more packing and I sat outside. She ordered me a great dinner that evening, I remember – it was little braised birds in gravy and, as I chomped into them, I imagined it was those nasty pigeons I was eating. Sheila went off for her naughty cocks tails, I suppose with Juan, and then when she returned from dinner she said we were all going to see a really good musical show ... music we all liked by beetles. Beetles? The only beetles I've ever seen just make the odd grating squeak when I crunch them; I never knew they were musical. Oh well, as I've said before, you learn something new every day! But if it was beetles AND good mewsic, well bring it on! We got to the theatre early but even so it was packed and there were people standing. Juan and Sheila were lucky and got seats and I perched on Juan's lap peering down at the stage below. His thighs weren't so fat and comfortable as Sheila's.

Well, everybody but everybody just loved the beetles' sound. I could see four guys on the stage, three playing geetars (not sure I spelt that right!) and one was banging on drums. They were all singing, though they certainly didn't sound like the beetles in our garden at home. The people watching were singing along too and some were dancing in between the lines of seats. Even Sheila and Juan were humming along to the tunes. At the end of the show, Sue came on stage and asked if we wanted more. Yes, we did! So they carried on with two more songs and then after more shouting and cheering they eventually were allowed to go off the stage.

"Well," said Sheila to Juan, "they were almost as good as the genuine article."

"Yes," he agreed, "come on, we'll go and have a coffee, Hanns knows now exactly how I like it!"

"And," said Sheila, "he's generous with my Amoretto too!" And so, we got up and followed the crowd of people out of the theatre.

Afterwards, we were on the way back 'home' and Sheila suddenly stopped and said, "I know it's late but Misty, it's nearly the end of the cruise, I'm going to the casino just one more time to see if I can still get lucky!" So, she dragged me all the way back again … the casino was very crowded so I guess other people must have thought the same. We had to walk up and down before we found a machine with nobody using it. "Oh look," laughed Sheila, "it's called Cats – it only plays cents so even if I lose it's not exactly going to break the bank!" With a resigned sigh I settled down at her feet and she put in her money and began pushing buttons making lots of little pictures of cats whizz round and round. As usual sometimes she won, sometimes she lost, but then, as had happened before, the machine started making loud mewsic and then she was grinning from ear to ear as she had ended up with 19,000 cents! Wow, were we rich? I wondered – maybe I could have a diamond collar now! As if she could read my thoughts, Sheila leaned down, laughed and said that I shouldn't get too excited, in fact it was only $190 but with the rest she'd won she would go home with a profit. Result! So we strolled happily back, she finished her packing and we eventually got to bed at about 2.30 a.m. in the morning. Sleep soon overcame both of us.

DAY 14

Oh dear, the last day. It wasn't very hot on the balcony this morning and the blue sky had turned grey. Oh well, back to normality! I ate my breakfast slowly and then Sheila left for hers and Del came in.

"Ello, Mistee, I'm so sorree to say goodbye to you." Me too, Del, I thought, you've been great. "Two shreemps today, Mistee, as I won't see you tomorrow morning," he said. Oh, purr, purr, purr Del! I sat and watched him do his chores and then he picked me up and stroked me … then he was gone. Did I see a tear in his eye? Aaah! When Sheila returned she looked sad as well.

"Oh well, Misty," she said, "just one day and it'll be ME doing the cleaning and making the bed. Come on, let's go and make the most of it." Too right, I thought, so it was on with the lead and off we went. At least I wouldn't have to wear that again after we got home! First stop was to the big lounge at the top for the final of the question game and the rest of the Sea Legs team didn't look too cheery either. Nobody wanted to go home after the lovely time they'd had. Sheila said she would ask if she could help with the cleaning so she could stay on (laughs all round!). I know ships in the old days used to employ cats to catch mice (the thought of doing a job like that made my mouth water!) and I wondered if I could apply here, but there again, on this spotlessly clean ship there certainly weren't any mice that needed catching. So that idea was out … more's the pity!

I sat and idly watched all the people passing by and then, as before, the atmosphere in the room got very tense and petite Sam reminded everyone that this was the final so the first three teams would win prizes and she wished good luck to everyone. Over the next half hour there were lots of questions, lots of shouts and lots of arguing amongst all the team members. In the end, team Sea Legs had moved up to fourth place so they just missed out on getting a prize. But they seemed pleased with their efforts and when we said our goodbyes, I got lots of pats and promises that they would read my book (this book!) when it came out.

Next stop was to the lower deck and there seemed to be another question game going on there – this time it must have been about food because Darran with the big white hat was there getting people to try their hands at cooking different dishes. Sheila watches something like this at home on the TV and it's called Master Chef I think (so it's not only dogs who have masters!). The Amerrycan people were calling it 'Top Chef' – so I could be on that game I think … Top Cat would definitely win Top Chef! But we didn't stop to watch and carried on until we came to where the shops were. Oh no, not more shopping surely! But Sheila miraculously passed by the shops and we ended up in the open space outside the noisy disco – which wasn't noisy now.

"I might have a treat for you now, Misty," Sheila said and I could see people were playing that game where you tap a little white ball with a long stick and get it into a hole, though here it wasn't going into a hole but a kind of box. This looked interesting, yes, and I remembered on the last trip I had been the winner when we had played the same game, but outside. It was dead easy for me to flick the ball into the holes with my paw, just like when I pat snails into holes in the flower beds at home, so I'd had plenty of practice. I looked up at Sheila and hoped she would let me have a go.

And yes, this was the treat she had mentioned! When there was a pause between games, she asked Tim, who was in charge of things, if I could have a go so I could show everyone how I could get a hole in one. Laughs from the people nearby.

"Why not?" he said, "she'll never be able to do that, surely!"

"Bet you an Amoretto coffee she will," said Sheila.

"Come on then, Misty" he said. Well, Tim, the laugh will be on you this time I thought, not on me! Sheila let me off the lead telling me that I was not to run off, and then Tim threw a ball in front of me. Paw out, ball hit and straight into the box it went! Cheer from the people watching. Oh yes, I liked this – being in the limelight. Tim chucked the ball again and this time, and I admit I was showing off, I turned around and kicked it straight into the hole with my back paw. Laughs and shouts from the watchers and people got out their picture making machines. I repeated the performance four more times, using different paws and never once missed. Well, I knew I wouldn't. Tim was flabbergasted. Sheila clapped her hands and told him that after the treadmill fiasco she knew I would redeem myself with my putting skills.

"Well Misty" he said, leaning down and patting me, "you certainly did that and you've well and truly taken the wind out of my sails." What on earth is he on about now? I thought, sails, wind? Oh well, whatever! "See you after lunch for that Amoretto coffee then," laughed Sheila and dragged me off towards the shops.

Shopping, as you will have realised, is not my thing but I was feeling quite upbeat after my ball in the hole game so, as I knew this would be the last time for her on this trip, I didn't begrudge Sheila her own treat. She didn't go too mad, no more bags or teddies just more chocolates, some of that sickly smelling stuff you spray on your necks and a ring, not a diamond one though!

After lunch we met up with Tim in the coffee lounge and he did keep his promise and buy Sheila an Amoretto coffee and then another ... she's doing well with those today, I thought, and we haven't even got to the evening yet! I sat between them and he patted me and said he couldn't believe how good I was at golf. Ah, Tim, full of surprises that's me! Tim looked smart again dressed in a nice shirt (though not as trendy as the ones Juan wears) and smart trousers (though not as form fitting as Maarten's) but he did beat the others when it came to flashy cufflinks. He reminded me a bit of Michael (aka Mr Pumpkin) who I met on the last cruise as, like Mr P, he had shaved off not only his face fur, but also his head fur. It seems the fashion for you men now to get rid of your head fur but I have seen a few more of you lately leaving your face fur as it should be ... which is something I suppose!

It seemed Tim was looking smart because later in the afternoon he was going to help Maarten host a singing session with a group of passengers who had formed a choir (that's something like our cats' chorus at home I think, but I shouldn't think it would sound as good!). He said to Sheila that he was surprised she hadn't joined the choir too but she replied that she sang like a pig with asthma. Well, that's pretty well true dear! Whilst they chattered on, I thought how much you could do on a cruise – learn to cook, play all manner of outdoor and indoor games, learn to dance, sing, listen to interesting talks, relax in the spa, go to sales, give away your money to the casino ... the list was endless. Not that Sheila ever did much except drink coffee! Still, there was something for all tastes – lazy people like her(!) or active ones! When we parted, Tim arranged to contact Sheila when he was next back home in Cornwall, gave me a final pat and off we went and spent the next hour just wandering about and saying goodbye to her passenger friends on board. Everyone looked a bit sad that they were going home. Not least us!

Then we met up with China boy Peng Fei again. I was so pleased he had survived the cruise without breaking into pieces. Sheila showed him the pack of cat cards. "Bet you've not seen a pack like that," she said, "no hearts, spades, diamonds or clubs, but just lots of cats!"

"No I haven't," he said. Then Sheila showed him the game and they played it for a while, laughing as before. I'm not quite sure why they seemed to find cats so funny.

"I suppose you're going to do a trick with them now," said Sheila.

"Of course!" he replied. He had fooled me before with a magic trick with cups and balls which, despite my sharp eyes, I just had not been able to solve. I was determined he wouldn't fool me with this card trick too so I sat watching with both eyes peeled. He took the pack of cards and asked Sheila which cat would she like. She said a Birman because we used to have a Birman in the family, called Taro. Peng Fei found the Birman card and gave it to Sheila. "Now, put it anywhere in the pack and get Misty to push the cards about and muddle them all up," he said putting them down on the floor in front of me. So she put the Birman card in somewhere and I pawed them all into a rather messy heap. I never took my eyes off them and he picked up the cards and then opened the pack about halfway revealing a card but it was of a black cat, NOT a Birman! Oooh, he's made a mistake at last, I thought!

"No, that's not the one," agreed Sheila.

"Oh dear," laughed Peng Fei, "Misty, push off the top card please." I did and, of course, it was the Birman! How does he do these things – and so quickly too? I sat back again and started to ankle watch as they talked for a few more minutes. It seemed that Peng Fei was also leaving the ship tomorrow and going home. He'd had even more stuff to pack than Sheila – with all the things he used for his shows in the theatre. Hugs all round, they both said they'd keep in touch and off we went.

It seemed a bit flat now it was the last night. Both Sheila and I walked rather sadly back to the stateroom and she sat down and put on the TV news but didn't really pay much attention to it. I partook of my litter box but didn't stay outside as the grey clouds outside didn't look very attractive. My last supper was duck and orange pate followed by salmon so I made it last as long as possible as tomorrow it would be back to supermarket own brands again. Still, I'd had a second taste now of shipboard life and how the other half lived, and had experienced something that no other cat I know would ever do. I felt I would definitely be doing a bit of bragging when I saw them next. Sheila had decided not to go to the show tonight so we just met Juan as usual in the Passport Bar. He was going to the show as it was a man singer he wanted to see. Well, he is very fond of good music. Sheila agreed we'd meet up with him later to say goodbye and they could drink their final Amoretto coffees. Bet she won't tell him she's had about four already, I thought! So, all we did then was to have a final wander round the shops and then went and said goodbye to Darren and Guy, who said it would be a CATastrophe if we never met again, to which Sheila replied that she had already booked from next year's CATalogue and would see them again in May! Back later to the stateroom and she heaved her three cases and my large bag outside the door where they would be picked up later and the next time we would see them would be when we got off the ship in Southampton docks. I noticed that the people in the next room had one case between the two of them!

Then we met up with Juan and it was quite sad really because he had been so nice and friendly and good company. Still, he and Sheila agreed to keep in touch by the wonders of email (not sure what that is, but I don't think the postman brings it to the house with the rest of our mail) and he said he might come and visit Cornwall one day when he was on his travels. Then Sue passed by and there were more goodbyes. Seeing her shoes close up I reckoned that I probably could have got underneath them, but thought I'd better not as she might fall over and not be able to climb back up on them again. I could see Sheila taking the odd sneaky peek at them and admiring them. But as

I said before, she'd never be able to take two steps in them. Then it was the final goodbyes to Hanns and Randy, again hugs all round and off we went … the end of a purrfect cruise!

I'm not going to bore you with the details of getting off the ship and going home – those of you who have read my previous book will have heard it all before. Suffice to say all went well and we had a good trip home, no probs! All I will say is that I hope you've enjoyed my sea cat's (b)log and those of you who have been on this lovely ship will recognise it from my description and it will make you smile and remember. To those of you who have not read my first book about cruising, or my predecessor, Truffles' book, and who have not tried a cruise yourselves, well please DO so! I can CATegorically recommend it! Bye, ciao, adios, au revoir, arrivederci … Misty xxx

ABOUT THE AUTHOR

Sheila Collins was born and brought up in Croydon. She attended Selhurst Grammar School and then went on to Croydon Technical College where she completed a one year secretarial course. During the years that followed Sheila held various secretarial/PA posts at managerial and directorial levels in London, Bournemouth and, latterly, in Cornwall, where she lives now. In recent years she has channelled her word power into the successful humour of the Truffles' Diaries series of books and both Truffles' and now Misty's adventures at sea. Being a lover of dogs as well as cats, she has also produced several other pet orientated books. Sheila holds a diploma in illustration and cartooning, a skill she puts to good use, though in Misty's books there are no actual illustrations, just a charming picture of her (Misty, not Sheila!) on the front cover. This is Sheila's tenth published book from Apex Publishing. She lists her pleasures in life as the 'Three C's'... cats, cruising and chocolate – in no particular order.

www.ingramcontent.com/pod-product-compliance
Lightning Source LLC
Chambersburg PA
CBHW022038170626
46808CB00003B/1255